ENCHANTED EVENING

Lynnette Hallberg

Chivers Press • G.K. Hall & Co.
Bath, England   Waterville, Maine USA

This Large Print edition is published by Chivers Press, England, and by G.K. Hall & Co., USA.

Published in 2001 in the U.K. by arrangement with the Author c/o Dorrie Simmonds.

Published in 2001 in the U.S. by arrangement with Kensington Books, an imprint of Kensington Publishing Corporation.

U.K. Hardcover   ISBN 0-7540-4560-9   (Chivers Large Print)
U.K. Softcover   ISBN 0-7540-4561-7   (Camden Large Print)
U.S. Softcover   ISBN 0-7838-9474-0   (Nightingale Series Edition)

The text of this Large Print edition is unabridged.
Other aspects of the book may vary from the original edition.

Set in 16 pt. New Times Roman.

Printed in Great Britain on acid-free paper.

British Library Cataloguing in Publication Data available

Library of Congress Cataloging-in-Publication Data

Hallberg, Lynnette, 1949–
        Enchanted evening / Lynnette Hallberg.
            p.   cm.
        ISBN 0-7838-9474-0 (lg. print : sc : alk. paper)
        1. Women lawyers—Fiction. 2. Physicians—Fiction.
        3. Large type books. I. Title.
        PS3558.A3783 E54 2001
        813'.6—dc21   2001024203

ENCHANTED EVENING

Love to my guys, Dave, Aaron, and Dad and to my Heavenly angels, Mom and Brian. Sue and Jim, love eternal.

CHAPTER ONE

Brianna Winters figured she had seven hundred and eighty-three minutes to live. So where was a girl's fairy godmother when she needed her?

Bri's old black cat twined himself around her leg. She knelt and rested her head against his, stroking his soft fur.

'Got any ideas, J.C. ?'

The cat meowed softly.

She grabbed the note she'd scribbled off to her best friend and dashed out the door. Once at the office, she'd stick it in an envelope and mail it.

Heavy lilac blooms bobbed and swayed by her front door. Their sweet scent drifted to her. She plucked one and waved it in front of her nose as she hurried to her treasured '74 Karmann Ghia, one of the last made.

Friday had finally arrived. Her time was up.

*   *   *

Chase Mitchell checked his watch. Ross wouldn't be here for at least another ten minutes. All the psychology books said the eldest sibling tended to be the responsible one.

Yet Chase was still waiting for his oldest brother. Again. Maybe next Friday *he'd* come

1

ten minutes late. No, make that twenty. Let Ross wait for him outside Madge's Restaurant. He smiled. Yeah, he liked that idea.

And then every thought of his brother fled.

A pair of legs like none he'd ever seen broke his line of vision. And the woman they belonged to was in one heck of a hurry. His head jerked up; his mouth dropped open. The package was complete.

The woman stood poised on the edge of the sidewalk, while she waited for a break in traffic. A cardinal red suit hugged an hourglass figure. Its slim skirt skimmed the tops of her knees and revealed legs any model would envy.

Chase freed his hands from his jeans pockets. Sunlight gleamed in the straight, silky strands of her pale blond hair and made it look like a golden waterfall. Then she turned. The full impact of her beauty nearly dropped him to his knees.

He pushed away from the building as the light changed. Spellbound, he watched her dash across the busy street.

A single sheet of paper fell from a notebook tucked in the crook of her arm, drifted down, and glided to a stop at the edge of the curb.

Chase pounced on the spot of pastel pink. Wild roses bordered neat rounded script written with an old-fashioned fountain pen. He raised the letter toward his nose, harboring the hope that it held her scent. It did. A rich, floral fragrance rose to tease him. Vibrant. Bold.

Feminine. It matched the red suit and its wearer. His gaze slid to the bottom of the page and focused on her name.

Brianna.

The name floated through his mind, delicate, elegant, fairylike.

He raised his head in time to see the red suit disappear inside a venerable, ten-story building. Its marble façade bore a polished brass plaque engraved with three names: Bradbury, Bradbury, and Haines. The prestigious Pittsburgh law firm had called the building home for the last century. Chase's brother, Ross, had once considered a position with them when he'd finally passed the bar.

The light changed again. Impulsively, he raced after the woman, darting between cars. Caution went out the window.

Catching his breath, he stepped into the revolving door and exited inside the foyer. Its high ceiling and marble floor created an echoing hollowness. Then he heard the telltale ping of the elevator as the door opened. Before he could call to her, the woman stepped inside, the door closed, and the elevator whisked her away.

He leaned against the cool plaster wall and tipped his head back, eyes closed in frustration. One hand jammed deep into the pocket of his faded blue jeans, he turned back toward the highly polished elevator door. The lights above it recorded her ascent, measured the distance she traveled away from him. Second floor, third, fourth, fifth. It stopped.

Did she work on the fifth floor or had it paused to let someone on, someone who now stood in that small, enclosed space with her, enjoying her warm, flowery scent? He closed his eyes again and swallowed hard. He needed to get a life.

'Excuse me. Is there something I can help you with, sir?'

The crisp, no-nonsense voice jolted him. Chase swiveled on his heels, the gray marble beneath his shoes slippery and smooth. A receptionist in her mid fifties sat at a sedate cherry desk and stared at him over reading glasses. A chain dangled from them. Her right hand cupped the mouth of the telephone receiver.

'Pardon?' Chase's voice sounded rusty and unused.

'I said, may I help you?' She enunciated each word carefully and clearly, the way a teacher spoke when asking a young child why he had misbehaved. He had, quite obviously, entered this woman's domain.

He nodded his head toward the bank of elevators. 'The woman . . . the one who just came in . . .'

'Ms. Winters?'

'Yeah, Ms. Winters.' Chase felt the play of a faint smile at the edge of his lips. Winters. Now he had a last name.

4

Then his smile disappeared. She was lovely, vibrant, alive. The cold name didn't fit her. And yet, at the same time, it suited her perfectly. When he looked at her, he felt the way he did when he first stepped out into a sunny winter day. That moment that stole your breath away. When everything seemed clearer, crisper, on the edge. Yeah, he decided, he liked the name. Brianna Winters.

'Sir?'

He turned his attention back to the receptionist. 'Hmmm?'

'Do you have an appointment? Shall I let Ms. Winters know you're here?'

'No.' He hesitated a moment. 'Yes.'

Just as fast, he changed his mind again. 'No.'

He glanced at the copper nameplate on the desk. 'No, Mrs. Burton, I'll call her later.' He checked his watch. 'I'm running late for another appointment.' Shaking her head, the receptionist picked up a pen. 'That's fine.'

Dismissing him, she returned to her phone call.

Chase stepped into the revolving door. It was past time to meet his brother. Once on the street, he remembered the letter clutched in his right hand. Should he ask Mrs. Burton to deliver it to her?

Morality and curiosity battled it out.

Curiosity won hands-down. While he waited for the light to change, he stood at the curb

5

and read the clean, compact handwriting.

Reeny,

Where are you when I need you? Don't tell me. I know. You're soaking up sun on that little tropical island you found, salt water and sand oozing between your toes. I'm dying to talk to you. Promise me your next vacation will be somewhere that has phones in the hotel rooms.

No doubt you're keeping an eye on some good-looking beach boy. Too bad you can't stick a stamp on him and mail him to me. Sure would get me out of a jam.

I've really done it this time, friend. Tonight's it. The moment of reckoning.

At eight o'clock sharp, I'm expected to show up at my law firm's annual charity ball. Wonderful, huh? They'll raise a gazillion dollars. Everybody, but everybody, will be there.

Which brings me back to my problem. While everyone sips champagne and eats caviar, I'll dine on crow. They'll be there dripping in their diamonds and sequins . . . and expecting to meet my fiancé. The ultimate romantic. Prince Charming personified. The hunk who swept me off my feet.

The man who doesn't exist!

What am I going to do, Reeny? I have to go to this thing. Nothing short of Mom showing up with my death certificate will work as an

6

excuse. And even then, they'd probably demote me to the job of assistant to the junior assistant!

What was I thinking when I promised to bring him tonight? I'm so darned tired of everybody setting up poor old Bri with their mother's sister's cousin's son. You know?

Guess I'll have to walk into that room of vultures alone and throw myself on their mercy.

Do you think there is such a thing as 'rent-a-fairy-godmother?' You know, like a 'rent-a-cop?' I could definitely use some magic, Reeny.

> *Woefully yours,*
> *Brianna*

P.S Can you believe we're going to turn thirty this month? Your birthday gift is wrapped and on the top shelf of my bedroom closet. If I decide to run away to Mexico or some other foreign country between now and eight o'clock, be sure Mom gives it to you. You'll love it. I know, 'cause I liked it so much I used it and had to buy another one for you.

Next time you talk to your mom, tell her I send my love.

A whistle escaped Chase. So, the lady needed a date for an important party. Tonight. But why? That gorgeous female couldn't come up with a date? She must have some hidden flaw. Still . . .

* * *

'You're late!'

Chase strolled over to their usual corner table. 'You were late, too.'

'Yeah, but you're later.' Ross chortled and tapped his watch.

Refusing to rise to the bait, Chase dropped into the chair and pulled a coffee cup toward him. He caught the waitress's eye. 'Morning, Madge. Think I'll have a cup of the real stuff today.'

He set the letter on the table, facedown. 'What's the name of that Disney animated movie, the one where the girl wants to go to the big dance?'

Silence met his question. Ross didn't watch movies with no violence, Chase remembered, and Madge didn't seem to be listening.

'Come on, you know. The pumpkin takes her.'

Behind him a tiny voice chirped, 'Cinderella.'

Chase turned and came eye to eye with the cutest little charmer he'd ever met. Four or five years old, she bashfully twirled on the heels of her shiny black patent leather shoes.

Chase smiled. 'Yeah, that's it. Cinderella.'

'And the mices and doggie went, too. Her fairy godmother comed and made her

8

beautiful, only she was already. And the fairy said some magic words and waved her magic wand and all of a sudden, poof!' The little girl waved her hands in the air, mimicking the fairy's motions. 'Cinderella's dress turned into a pretty blue one. Just like that.'

'Emily, come over here and sit down. Leave those men alone.' The child's mother threw an apologetic look at the two. 'Sorry.'

'It's okay. She's been a big help.' Chase watched the tiny girl scramble onto her chair and scoop up a bite of pancake.

'I helped him, Mommy.' The words came out around a mouthful of breakfast.

'Yes, you did, sweetheart.'

Chase felt his brother's eyes on him. 'What?'

'That's what I want to know, baby brother. What's all this with the fairy tales?'

'Nothing.' He shrugged. 'I wondered. That's all.'

'Uh uh. No way.' Ross eyed the piece of pink stationery and grabbed for it. 'It has something to do with this note, doesn't it?'

Chase batted his hand away. 'Leave it be, okay?' he growled.

Madge filled his cup to the top. 'You thinking of playing Prince Charming for somebody?'

'No,' he said. 'What the hell makes this Prince Charming so special anyway?'

'Oooh, you said a naughty word. Didn't he,

Mommy?' The wide-eyed little girl knelt backward in her chair and regarded Chase.

He blushed. For the life of him, he couldn't remember the last time he'd done that. But this tiny tot disarmed him.

'I did. And I'm sorry. Shame on me.' He met her mother's amused eyes and raised his brows. 'Hope she doesn't repeat that at preschool.'

'I won't. I never use naughty words, do I, Mommy? If you do, Miss Sandy makes you sit in the little chair while the other kids play.' She spoke so solemnly that Chase felt even more ashamed.

With that, she turned back to her pancakes and drowned them in syrup.

Chase took another gulp of coffee, then cleared his throat. 'So, Madge, what exactly is expected of Prince Charming?'

'He is the fulfillment of a woman's dreams. He is fantasy come true. He's romance. He's gallantry. He's . . . the best!'

'Is that all?' Cynicism filled his voice. 'Hel . . .' He felt the little girl's eyes on his back. 'I mean, gee, that should be easy enough.'

Madge looked him up and down and slowly nodded. 'Yep, you've got all the basic equipment. Blond hair, nice white teeth, cute dimples, wide shoulders. You're tall enough, too. The eyes really should be blue, but I guess green will do.' Her own narrowed. 'Stand up, and let me look at your butt.'

10

'My . . . I will not!'

She threw her hands up in defeat. 'I can't be sure, then, can I?'

Deciding to play along, he shifted his long legs from beneath the table and stood, turning his backside to her. Clad in tight fitting jeans, he figured she'd get a good look.

'You'll do.' She swatted his behind with her dishtowel. 'Sit down now, and tell me what you want to eat.'

'I'll do? That's it?'

'Yep.'

Slightly offended, he decided he'd have liked a somewhat more flattering reply, but knew it wouldn't come from Madge. Close to sixty, she'd surely seen her share of backsides.

'I'll do,' he muttered again.

He dropped back into his chair, then groaned when he saw the pink stationery in his brother's hand. He swiped the letter from Ross.

Determined to ignore the twinkle in his eyes, Chase asked, 'What's the special this morning, Madge?'

Then he groaned again. He'd placed the note face up and Madge leaned over his shoulder, unabashedly reading it. When she finished, she reeled off the specials and took their orders.

'Seems to me the best special might not be on the menu today, though.' She tipped her head at the note he held and then walked off

11

toward the kitchen.

He grimaced. Every Friday he and Ross met here for breakfast. Madge and her husband, who owned the place, dished up the best basic food in the Pittsburgh area. From the look in his brother's eye, Chase figured Ross was cooking up something of his own, and he'd bet dollars to donuts it didn't have a thing to do with food.

'So? Are you going to do it?' Ross reached for the sugar and dumped two spoonfuls into his coffee.

'That much sugar's not good for you. Am I going to do what?' Chase took a drink of his black coffee and straightened the silverware on his place mat.

'Go with Brianna to this thing tonight.'

'Absolutely not.' He pushed to the back of his mind the fact that he'd considered it. 'I don't know her. She's twenty-nine and can't get a date. What does that tell you?'

'That she's discriminating?'

'No,' Chase countered. 'Something has to be seriously wrong with her, even though you wouldn't know it to look at her.'

Madge came to their table with a selection of jams and jellies, two plates of toast juggled in her other hand. 'So, what are the two of you up to tonight?'

Ross jumped in. 'I promised a friend from the office I'd help her pick out a new stereo system for her apartment.'

'Chase? What about you?'

There it was. The question he'd dreaded. The two of them had ganged up on him.

Ross slathered an entire container of strawberry jam on a piece of toast, smiled, and answered for him. 'He just might be going to a ball, Madge. With Cinderella, no less.'

Madge set down her coffeepot and slid onto a chair between the two men. 'Tell me about her, Chase.'

His stomach dropped. Another matchmaker. Heaven save bachelors from them all. With a resigned sigh, he explained the note and how he'd come to have it.

'Are you going to take her?' Madge's eyes gleamed with the prospects of this new romance.

'No!'

Two pairs of eyes bored into him, all but accused him of some horrible crime.

'What?' He squirmed under their scrutiny. 'No way. And I don't have to give a reason why.'

'Madge, why don't you give me a few minutes alone here with my little brother? Come back in five with a coffee refill.'

Before she was even out of hearing, Chase turned to Ross. In a vehement whisper, he said, 'Stay out of this. I'm not into blind dates. Been there, done that. And I'm sure as hell no Prince Charming.'

'I agree. You're not. So, what *are* you doing

13

tonight?'

'Nothing.'

'Well, then, what have you got to lose?'

'Are you crazy?' Chase pulled back in his chair and stared at his older brother as though he'd grown a second head.

Ross's smile slid away. 'Seriously. Why not?'

'I can't.'

'Chase, I'm the one who lost Jane . . .'

'No.' Angry eyes raised to meet his brother's. His instincts cried out, warned him to stay clear of Brianna Winters.

But Ross remained obstinate. 'It's only for one night, right?'

'Yeah.'

'You saw her already. So even if she's uglier than sin, you're prepared for it.'

'Ugly?' Chase pictured again the blond hair, the legs, the curvy body in the red suit. He grew warm.

Madge saved him by setting his breakfast in front of him. He grumbled his thanks and speared a chunk of potato on his fork, then popped it into his mouth.

'She's not ugly, is she?' Ross badgered. 'I can tell by the look on your face. So just how gorgeous is she?'

Chase didn't answer. He scowled instead and carefully cut the fat off the edge of his ham. He shouldn't be eating this stuff. Just looking at it was enough to raise his cholesterol.

14

But Ross wasn't deterred. 'Maybe she's busy—like you. Maybe she has no time for dating.'

Chase ignored him and bit into his toast.

'I dare you.' The words fell onto the table between them, taunting, challenging.

'That's not fair.' Chase pointed his fork at his brother. 'You know that's not fair.' He stabbed another bite of ham. 'I hate it when you do this.'

Ross laughed. The rich sound filled the small eatery. 'Can't resist, can you? Tell you what. You take the princess to her ball tonight, and I'll buy breakfast for the next two weeks.'

Chase chewed the ham, counted to ten, then twenty. 'I don't want to.'

'You're afraid to.'

'I am not.'

'Are, too.' After the space of a heartbeat, Ross said, 'I'll buy the next *four* weeks.'

Tossing his fork down, Chase rubbed the bridge of his nose, defeated. He'd never in his life been able to resist a dare, and Ross knew it.

'Fine. But I'm ordering steak and eggs every single week, cholesterol be damned.' He remembered the little girl behind him. 'Sorry. Cholesterol be darned.'

Then he glared across the table. 'It's going to cost you.'

He tipped his cup and drained the last of the hot, black brew.

15

As if on cue, Madge showed up to provide a refill. Curious, she looked from one to the other.

'Yes, Madge. I'll do it. One date. Period. There isn't going to be any happily-ever-after. Got it?'

She leaned over and patted his cheek. 'You're a good boy, Chase Mitchell. Your mama must be awfully proud of you.'

Straightening, she tied her apron more firmly around her waist. 'One more thing.'

She tapped the innocent looking letter that had started all the commotion. 'I know Brianna. She comes in here for lunch when she remembers to eat.'

Oh, oh. Here it comes, Chase thought. *This is where she drops it on me. The reason Brianna has no date.*

'You have to be more than a casual date tonight, according to this. You're her fiancé, right?'

Even the thought filled him with dread. He knew it showed because Ross took one look at him and sprayed coffee with a muffled laugh. Chase enjoyed watching him choke as the liquid went down the wrong pipe.

'Yeah. So?'

'Well, keep in mind that you're pretending.'

'That doesn't sound too bad, Chase.' A bad-boy grin flashed across Ross's face.

Madge read his meaning and rounded on Chase again. 'You pretend you're her fiancé at

16

the ball; then you take her home, shake hands good night, and that's that. No fooling around. Brianna's a nice girl.'

'I'm sure she is.' Chase massaged his forehead where the beginning of a headache danced. What had Ross goaded him into this time? And when would he learn?

He picked up the letter and folded it, then stuffed it into his pocket. 'I'll need this. Her address is on it.'

When he looked back at Madge, she winked.

CHAPTER TWO

Dried mud cracked, forming little spider webs on Brianna's face. Draped across the bed, comfortable in a tattered old blue robe, she closed her eyes, and listened to her sister on the other end of the phone. J.C. curled at her feet, his purr comforting. Absently, she stroked his head.

'You can't come up with a single emergency, Allie? Come on. Be creative.'

Brianna listened to her stepsister's reassurances, then said, 'Easy for you to say. You're not the one walking into the shark tank tonight. Alone.'

Dread seemed to have taken up permanent residence in the pit of her stomach.

The doorbell rang.

'Hold on a sec. Someone's at the door.'

Pulling her robe closer around her, she walked to the front door and peered out. A delivery boy stood on her porch, a florist's box in his hands.

She opened the door. 'Yes?'

'Brianna Winters?'

'Yes.'

'For you.' He handed her the flowers.

Nonplussed, she took them, opened the box, and read the card. Her forehead creased in a frown at the cryptic message.

'Who sent these?'

The teenager shrugged. 'I don't know. Why?'

'This note says they're from my fairy godmother. That Prince Charming is coming to take me to the ball.'

The boy stepped back. 'Sure, lady. And I gotta get out of here before I change into a pumpkin or a rat or somethin'.' He turned to leave.

'Wait,' she called. 'Let me get some money for you.'

He waved the offer aside. 'Don't bother.' His gaze flicked from her mud-caked face to her ragged robe. 'Looks like you need it more than I do.'

Flustered, she closed the door and rushed back to the phone.

'Allie? You won't believe this.' Bri blurted

18

out what had just happened.

'Well, sounds like you'd better go get beautiful. Be a shame to waste a Prince Charming. They're hard to find.' Allie laughed. 'Have a great time. I'll expect to hear all about it in the morning. Oh, and be in before midnight.'

Brianna held the phone to her chest after Allie hung up. What was going on?

Then she caught a glimpse of herself in the mirror, her facial masque cracked and peeling. The clock chimed seven. Oh, God, what if Prince Charming really showed up?

She hustled into the bathroom to scrub her face. Halfway done, water and brown ooze dripping from her chin, she leaned over the sink and laughed.

Honestly! There was about as much chance that Prince Charming would walk through her door as there was that Santa Claus himself would arrive accompanied by Rudolph and all seven of Snow White's dwarfs. She splashed more water over her face, then patted it dry with a soft towel.

But what if?

She flew into panicky action, dressing at warp speed. Hair done, makeup in place, she sat on the edge of the bed and reread the handwritten card that accompanied the gardenias. Their fragrance filled her living room and spilled into the bedroom.

Brianna,

Sorry for the note, but I don't do house calls anymore. Too old for all that appearing and disappearing stuff. Arthritis flares up with the molecular changes. Anyway, everything's taken care of. Prince Charming will arrive to pick you up at seven-thirty. Have fun.

Your Fairy Godmother

Fairy godmother! Wishful thinking! Brianna worried her bottom lip with her teeth. Who'd sent this?

Resentment seeped through her. Who wrote the rule that said she had to have a man to go with anyway? Why couldn't everyone deal with the fact that she wanted to manage her own life? She didn't need, didn't want, a man to lean on. A man to break her heart.

Her father's long-ago betrayal still shadowed her. She refused to depend on a man for her happiness, her security. Far safer to take care of herself. She could, and she would.

She read the note again. Obviously, someone felt differently.

She'd bet anything Allie was behind this. She probably sent the flowers to cheer her up. But her prince? What on earth was that all about?

Or had her stepfather sent them? Bernard had offered to escort her to the bash tonight, but she'd declined. Had he decided to show up

20

anyway?

Bri fastened her necklace, then stepped back to study her reflection in the mirror. No conservative little black dress for her tonight. No, sir. She'd had enough of listening to everyone's ideas of what she should and shouldn't do, should and shouldn't be, and the body-molding red dress suited her mood. Kind of like the one Scarlett wore to Ashley's birthday party, minus the feathers.

One foot slid into a two-inch heel as the doorbell pealed. One shoe on, the other in hand, she limped into the living room to answer it, certain her stepfather had arrived.

She threw the door open and stared, dumbstruck. The most gorgeous man she'd ever seen was standing on her front porch. Dressed in a black tux, a single red rose in hand, his blond hair glistened beneath her porch light.

Her breath rushed from her. If this was her prince, she owed her fairy godmother big time. She blinked. He was still there.

The tiny part of her brain that still functioned warned her he had to have the wrong address. No way was he here for her!

He opened the screen door. 'Brianna?'

She nodded wordlessly, unable to speak.

'Well, here I am.' He turned his wrist to check his watch. 'And on time, too. Heard we had a ball to attend. I'm yours for the night.' A hint of mischief laced the enigmatic words.

21

Yours for the night. The words echoed in her mind. Fantasies flew hot and heavy. She forced herself to ask, 'You're here to do what?'

Chase stood in the open doorway and simply stared at Brianna Winters. Her voice matched her appearance. She was a masterpiece of contradiction. Cool and contained. Hot and sexy.

Damn, but she was beautiful. Sheathed in a floor-length, ruby-red gown, she took his breath away. Literally. A sparkling red, dangerously high-heeled sandal dangled from one finger.

'The Wicked Witch of the West.'

'Excuse me?' She moved to close the door on him.

'Sorry. Sorry.' Palm flat against the door, he held it open. 'I think I have my fairy tales confused.'

Both her impeccably arched brows shot up, over the bluest eyes he'd ever seen. 'Look, I'm in a hurry. I have a very unpleasant appointment to keep. I don't mean to be rude, but I really don't have time to stand here discussing children's stories with you. So, if you'll move your hand . . .'

'Wait. Let me explain.' He watched as curiosity overcame impatience. 'You are Brianna Winters?'

'Yes, I am.' She glanced at *her* watch now. 'You have five seconds.'

Then she slapped her forehead. 'An escort.

Of course. You're a paid escort, aren't you? Someone hired you to go with me tonight.' A deep flush spread up her neck and over her face.

A paid escort? He bit back the retort that sprang instantly to mind. Then he remembered his brother's bet. Accepting a dare fell into a totally different category, even if a month's worth of Madge's breakfasts might be the payoff.

He tamped down his irritation. 'Look, I know a fairy godmother is supposed to appear in your garden, all sparkly and shimmery, but she couldn't make it. This is the best she could do.'

'I know. She has arthritis.' Brianna delivered the words dryly.

He frowned. Her remark didn't make sense. What was she talking about?

Bri went on. 'That's what her note said. The one that came with the beautiful gardenias.' She waved her hand toward the vase of flowers.

He nodded. Madge must have embellished the note they'd agreed on. He wondered what else she had added to it.

'Yeah, well,' she lost her magic wand, too. Maybe this can take its place.' He held the rose out to her.

Tentatively, she reached for it, then brought it to her face to enjoy its subtle fragrance.

Chase noticed she still held her other shoe.

He moved into action. This part he knew.

In one fluid motion, he removed the sandal from her finger and knelt. As he slid the shoe easily over her toes and onto her foot, his fingers caressed the silk-stockinged arch. He looked up to see Brianna staring open-mouthed at him.

He figured he might as well play his role to the hilt. 'It fits. That means you're the true princess, the one I dance the night away with.'

Eyeing the shoe, he shook his head. 'I thought it was supposed to be a glass slipper. Wasn't the ruby slipper the one Dorothy took away from the wicked witch in *The Wizard of Oz*?'

Brianna didn't answer Her delicate features still wore a slightly shell-shocked expression.

His voice lowered. 'You'll knock them dead tonight.'

Up until now, he hadn't decided quite how to proceed. His uncertainty dissolved. He would play the game the way it was written.

He wrapped her cold fingers in his. 'Prince Charming, at your service. Your fairy godmother sent me to take you to that ball.'

When she still didn't speak, he continued. 'Since the old gal has temporarily misplaced her magic wand, I'm afraid there's no crystal and gold carriage, no footmen. I think this should do, though.'

He stepped to the side to allow her a view of the street. Her eyes grew large at the sight of the shiny white limousine, a uniformed chauffeur beside it. This little extra had cost a bundle, but Ross and Madge both insisted she wouldn't go alone in an ordinary car with a stranger. They were probably right. Not with all the craziness in today's world. Although it could also be argued that lunatics drove around in limos just as often as anyone else.

'Who *are* you?' Her words held a slightly breathless, husky quality.

'Who do you want me to be?' The words fell between them, so soft they were almost a whisper. 'I'm your fantasy. *You* name me. I'm whomever and whatever you want me to be tonight.'

'Somebody paid you to take me to the ball, didn't they?' A trace of anger suffused her voice.

Hurriedly he denied the charge. 'No. Believe me, I'm not a paid escort.'

Even to his own ears, the words didn't sound quite credible. In a way, she was right. Chase fully intended to make Ross pay up, so in a way he was profiting from the night. But it wasn't the same as *being* paid.

Then why did he feel so guilty?

'Look. I'm here because you need me tonight. You and I are going to this company gala of yours, and we're going to bring your colleagues to their knees. We'll be the perfect couple.'

Her eyes narrowed. 'How do you know

about all this?'

'Fairy godmothers know everything.'

She snorted.

'Brianna, you need a fiancé. For tonight only. Here I am.'

'Right. Compliments of my fairy godmother.' Skepticism colored her words.

He ignored it and grinned. 'You got it, honey. Grab your bag or whatever you need, and let's do this place. On the way to the ball, you can fill me in on what I need to know—since we're about to be married.'

Brianna placed a hand over her stomach. His words filled her with a strange, silly fluttering. So she was about to be married. To a stranger. Prince Charming, no less. He sure did look the part, though.

She blew out a loud breath and struggled for control, afraid she might start to drool and ruin her new dress. Conflicting urges dueled within her. Should she barricade the door against this fantasy man and call 911—or grab her bag and go with him?

Her mind played Ping-Pong. Yes, she should go with him. After all, there was a driver, so they wouldn't be alone. No, she shouldn't. She didn't even know his name.

Yes, she should. Wasn't he the answer to her prayers? Maybe fairy godmothers really did exist. If so, hers must have worked overtime to find a guy this gorgeous.

Back and forth went the argument in her

mind.

If she agreed to this, she wouldn't have to walk alone into that room filled with coworkers.

What the heck? What could it hurt? One more night and then she'd tell everyone the truth.

But for right now, she'd enjoy the magic.

She started to turn. When his hand reached out and touched her bare back, she jerked away.

'Hold on. No need to be so skittish. I'm just going to finish zipping you up.'

Brianna heard the whisper of the zipper and remembered she'd had trouble with the last few inches. She chided herself for her nerves.

'Thanks,' she mumbled. 'Give me two minutes.' With that, she left him by the door and raced to her bedroom, praying she wouldn't regret this.

Mistake! The word ricocheted through Chase's mind. He watched as a last glimpse of red disappeared through the doorway, then rubbed a hand down the length of his face.

Everything about this gal screamed danger. A smart man would run for the limo—now— and tell the chauffeur to drive away. Fast and far. Self-preservation demanded it.

He didn't. Instead, he stepped farther into the living room. Interest piqued, he realized that the lady and the room seemed at odds. Which, he wondered, reflected the truth?

Brianna Winters, so sleek and sophisticated. So capable and career-minded. So far removed from this room that invited a person to put his feet up and relax. Everything about it said comfort; it whispered home. White wicker settee and chair with flowery cushions, white tables and bookcases, white paneled walls. Light and breezy. A sea of white dotted with bright splashes of color.

Every nook and cranny was filled. The bookcase by the window overflowed, its shelves crammed with books and magazines. He ran his finger along the spines. Gardening, romance, mystery, history, a real hodgepodge collection. The top of the case held framed photos, porcelain carousels, and a collection of glass paperweights.

Dried flowers spilled out of a basket on the floor by the coffee table and still more from another on the far side of the room. The gardenias Madge had ordered sat in the center of the hall table.

Everywhere his gaze landed, there was more stuff. The lady liked things, comfortable things, little doo-daddy things. Clean but cluttered, the room said a lot about Brianna.

A drift of floral scent announced her return.

Checking out a pile of magazines that practically hid an ottoman, he asked, 'Maid's day off?'

Then he raised his gaze to the lady in red. Red. Danger zone. Stop.

28

He couldn't.

One taste, he promised himself. One taste of her magic and no more.

Holding out his hand to her, they left without another word.

*   *   *

'Allie sent you, didn't she? No, it was my mother.' Brianna shook her head. 'No, it wasn't. Bernard must have arranged all this. Since I refused to let him take me, he pressed you into service.'

As she spoke, she fiddled with the controls of the console with one hand while she ran the other over smooth, rich leather upholstery. Then she opened the bar and checked out its contents.

Her mysterious prince silently watched her.

'You aren't going to tell me, are you?'

He shook his head.

'Okay.' She paused and then rushed on. 'Do you know Reeny? No, I lost her letter before I could even send it. Anyway, it wouldn't be there yet, so she didn't do this. I know, my mother knows your mother, and she asked you to do this, right?'

A single blond brow raised, his only acknowledgment of her questions.

She stared at the passing city blocks.

Finally, his voice filled the space between them. 'Look, Princess. There are a few things I

29

should probably know before we hit this gala together. After all, I think it's only fair to know a little bit about the woman who will be the mother of my children.'

The words jolted her. Even knowing he meant them as a joke, they still hit her hard.

When she raised her eyes to his, she blurted out the first thing that came to mind. 'I'm keeping my own checking account.'

To his credit, he tried to smother his surprised laugh in a fit of coughing. She closed her eyes. Embarrassment flooded her. Talk about old wounds surfacing.

'Sorry. Don't know why I said that.' Squinting, she fixed her eyes on him. 'You really do need a name, you know. I have to call you *something*.'

'What have you told everyone my name is?'

'Your name? You don't exist.'

'Actually, I do. I've been around for thirty-two years now. But what I mean is, when you talk to your coworkers about me, you must use some name.'

'Well, yes. I had to.' She smoothed the top of her hair. 'My fiancé's name is Chase. I never gave them a last name.'

Wariness hooded his expression. 'Chase? You told them my name was Chase?'

'Well, not yours exactly, but, yes.'

'That's a rather unusual name.'

She shrugged, and the red, off-the-shoulder dress shifted dangerously. 'I know. But I got so tired of everybody chasing around, trying to set me up with a guy. I figured I could chase them away if I came up with a man of my own. Voilà. The name. Chase.'

He swallowed and ran a finger beneath his black satin bow tie. 'Chase it is, then. Suits me fine.'

'So, what do you do, Chase?' She tried out the name and decided it fit.

'What do you want me to do?'

The first ten answers that came to mind earned an R-rating. Kissing, stroking, and like pursuits didn't really seem appropriate occupations, so she pushed them aside. 'I want you to be a doctor.'

His demeanor underwent another change. Suspicion flared in his eyes. He studied her intently for a moment before he answered. 'Fine. I'll be a doctor, then.'

Panic fluttered in her stomach at his easy acceptance. 'But what if someone asks you questions?'

With a twisted grin, he answered, 'Oh, I think I know enough about medicine to get by.'

'Okay, then. Here's the scoop. You've been out of town doing research. That's why I couldn't introduce you to people before.'

Pursing his lips, he nodded. 'And what about you? You're going to this bash thrown by the law firm. You obviously work there.'

'I'm a lawyer.'

31

His brows raised at that. 'Good for you. Brainy. I like that. We'll raise a brood of geniuses.' He smiled at the face she made. 'So, you live alone, and, from what I could see, you collect just about everything. You obviously don't have a cleaning lady, and you're going to keep your own checking account after we're married.'

Brianna felt the heated flush race up her neck.

His eyes sparkled with amusement. 'Anything else I should know? Do you scour dishes and floors? Dust your evil stepmother's and stepsister's bedchambers?'

She laughed. 'I don't have a stepmother, but I do have a stepfather.'

At his look of surprise, she continued. 'And one stepsister and a halfsister. But since my mom's still alive, she manages to keep them under control. Barely.'

She grinned easily at his stunned expression. 'See? I fit this role better than you realized.'

At his look of discomfort, she said, 'It's okay. My father died when I was ten. Mom remarried when I turned twelve, so Bernard's been in my life a long time. And I don't think anybody would call Allie and Shaylyn evil or ugly.'

'Allie?'

'Alexandra, actually. She's five months older than me. Shaylyn is thirteen years younger. So we're his, hers, and theirs.'

'Okay, then. My turn. Two brothers, Brett and Ross, both older; one sister, Ginny, five years younger; and one niece, Lainey. She's five. My mom and dad are both alive and still married to each other. I live alone. Well, sort of alone.'

'Sort of? Isn't that like sort of pregnant? You are, or you aren't? You do, or you don't?'

He laughed, a deep, rich sound. Dimples deepened beside his mouth. 'Okay, I don't live alone. But my roommates are the four-footed variety. I have two dogs. General George Armstrong Custer and Chief Sitting Bull, a yellow Lab and a bulldog. General and Bull for short.'

Time had run out. The car slid to the curb, and the driver came around to open the door for them.

The white limo stood as Brianna's last line of defense. The instant the door opened, the moment of reckoning would arrive.

Lights spilled into the night from the building's foyer. A few couples, dressed to kill in evening gowns and tails, lingered outside. Inside the car, not a sound could be heard. It was a little like watching a silent film or hitting the mute button on the TV remote.

Brianna experienced sheer terror. 'This can't possibly work!'

Chase leaned over and whispered in her ear, 'We'll make up the rest as we go. It'll be fine. Relax and enjoy yourself, Princess.'

He raised her hand to his lips and dropped a feather-light kiss into its palm. Brianna almost swooned.

She took a deep breath and prepared to step from the limo, her hand in his. For one fleeting moment, she imagined what it would be like if he were indeed her fiancé.

And then the thought fled. Reality set in. Like Cinderella, her dream would end with the day. When the clock struck twelve, she'd be back home—alone. In charge of her own life. Exactly the way she wanted it. But for now, she'd enjoy. If she could.

'They're going to know,' she whispered nervously. 'We can't possibly pull this off.'

'What's your favorite food?'

'My favorite food?'

He nodded.

'Asparagus and chocolate.'

At his look of horror, she added, 'Not together.'

'Phew. That's a relief. Don't worry. I'll take care of everything.'

She looked into his deep green eyes and believed him.

CHAPTER THREE

Chase winked at her. 'Okay, Princess, time to do it. Let's give 'em hell.'

34

The instant the limo door opened, noise bombarded them—a clash between the stillness that had cocooned them and the boisterousness of a party already in progress. Music, laughter, and unintelligible conversation spilled from the building.

He helped her from the car, but didn't release her hand once she stood on the sidewalk. When she tried to wrest it from him, he leaned into her.

'Let it go, Brianna. We're madly in love, remember? This is all part of the act.'

His breath warm on her face, his thumb played over the back of her hand. Rather than calm her, though, it added to her confusion and wreaked havoc with her already frayed nerves.

No novice to the game of love and romance, she'd done her share of hand-holding. What made it so different tonight? Why did Chase's touch send chills through her, followed so closely by a rush of heat? She suddenly wished she'd worn something looser. The slinky red dress didn't give her enough breathing room.

And then, she had no more time for thought.

Her law firm spared no expense on this annual event. The charity ball provided the partners of Bradbury, Bradbury, and Haines a chance to showcase their firm as a beneficent community asset, to counteract the negative publicity often generated by the daily press.

Local newspaper, radio, and television personalities had been invited. For the next week, photos, articles, and talk about the evening would pepper the media.

As Chase and Brianna walked toward the building, hand in hand, flashbulbs twinkled like stars and their entrance was captured on film. She fumbled for a smile, a look of calm happiness. She feared she achieved only dazed distress.

'Oh, my gosh, you look wonderful,' Stella, another lawyer at the firm, gushed. 'And you brought him! I'd about decided this hunk of yours was a figment of your imagination. Guess not, huh?' She fanned herself ineffectually with a cocktail napkin. 'Although he sure does look too good to be true.'

If you only knew, Brianna thought.

Remembering her manners, she made introductions. 'Chase, this is Stella Langsford. She and I work together on some of the firm's cases. Stella, my fiancé, Chase.' She stumbled over the last and prayed her coworker wouldn't notice the lack of a surname.

'Goodness, you're every bit as gorgeous as Brianna said.' Stella's lashes fluttered.

Wondering why her friend looked different tonight, Brianna leaned closer and realized she wore false lashes. One was a little out of line, giving her a slightly cross-eyed look. For one horrid moment, Brianna was afraid she might laugh.

That fear flew out the window when Chase raised his hand to her face and ran a finger along the curve of her jaw.

'Brianna's the gorgeous one.' Although he spoke to Stella, his eyes stayed fixed on Bri's so intensely, she actually sighed.

The sound shocked her out of her reverie. Nervous, she wet her lips, but didn't speak. She heard another sigh. This time it came from Stella. She tore her gaze from Chase's to stare at her friend, whose long-lashed eyes devoured her fiancé.

No, not her fiancé. Her blind date. One her unknown fairy godmother had somehow arranged for her. Could it have been—

'It was my mother, wasn't it?'

The instant she caught the questioning look in Stella's eyes, Brianna knew she'd inadvertently thought out loud. She looked desperately at Chase for help.

Chase, quick on his feet, covered for her with an outlandish fib. 'Sharp ears, Bri. I didn't even hear that page.' He checked the pager in his pocket for Stella's benefit. 'Just a friend calling. Your mother's fine, I'm sure.'

He leaned toward her and kissed her cheek, then brushed a stray lock of hair behind her ear. 'She worries too much, Stella.'

Her friend now openly gawked. Slightly breathless, she said, 'You got that right. We're always on her for that at the office.' A wave of her hand included all four hundred attendees.

'It doesn't matter what we're working on. Everything's done, ready to deliver, and Brianna has to give it one more go-through, just to be certain there's no language in the document or brief that could come back to haunt her client. I'll tell you, she worries herself to death.'

Bri opened her mouth to deny it, then halted. Stella was right. A stickler for detail, she relentlessly checked each and every one.

'Not tonight,' Chase vowed. 'Let's dance.'

Before she had time to think, Brianna found herself on the dance floor. Nothing could have prepared her for that instant when Chase pulled her into his arms. The man obviously had no concept of personal space. He drew her to him and rested his hand on her hip, tucked her into him until the full length of their bodies touched.

Brianna thought she'd surely died and gone to heaven. Resting her cheek against his shoulder, his scent tantalized her, made her weak-kneed. One of his hands remained on her hip. The other held hers next to his neck, their fingers entwined.

The band played a love song. She wanted it to last forever. She wanted it to end. She wanted not to want.

When that song ended, the live orchestra moved seamlessly into the next. Something slow and dreamy that she didn't recognize. Although she hadn't thought it possible, Chase snuggled her even closer into his body. The music, the soft lights, blurred in her mind. All she knew, all that existed, was this dangerous stranger, her Prince Charming. Her world began and ended right here in his arms. Nothing before this moment mattered.

Then his lips moved to her neck and he trailed whisper-light kisses up the length of it.

Flustered, she pulled back, her eyes meeting his. 'Don't do that.'

'It's window-dressing, sweetheart. Nothing more. People are watching. Nobody's going to buy this little charade of ours if we don't play our roles.'

She should have felt relief at the reminder. Instead, a flash of pain ripped through her heart.

His lips moved to her ear, his tongue warm on her flesh. She gasped and clung to him. And tried to remember that it was a game. A wish come true—temporarily. Nothing more.

It seemed so natural when his mouth claimed hers. She'd never tasted anything as exquisite, never needed anything more. Her hands moved to the back of his head. She buried her fingers in his hair, drew him closer still.

His lips left hers to travel over her cheek, up to her forehead. The kiss there left a brand, she was sure. He rested his face in her hair and swirled her across the dance floor.

Who was this man?

Game momentarily forgotten, she caught sight of a star shining in the sky outside the French doors and sent a wish drifting up to it. *Why can't he be more than a dream? Why does the fairy tale have to end?*

The magic ended abruptly. The real world intruded in the guise of one of the senior law partners who tapped Chase on the shoulder.

'Hate to do this to you two lovebirds, but I'm going to claim my dance with this beautiful lady. Brianna, you look wonderful tonight.'

He extended a hand to her escort and introduced himself. 'Lawrence Haines. And you must be the mysterious fiancé we've all heard so much about.'

'That I am. Glad to meet you, sir.' Chase exchanged a hearty handshake with the older, balding gentleman. His other arm stayed firmly around Brianna's waist.

Exerting pressure, he pulled her into his side and dropped a light kiss on her parted lips as though the thought of even this slight separation saddened him. 'Take good care of her.'

'Oh, I will.'

With that, Brianna found herself swung back onto the dance floor. The glow gone, she thudded back to earth. She and her boss chatted throughout the number.

When it ended, he said, 'I think I need a drink after that one. How about you?'

'Yes, I'd love something cold.'

He took her elbow and led her toward the far side of the room. A buffet table, loaded with delicacies of every kind, took up one long wall.

'Looks like your fellow found himself a friend while we were busy.' Lawrence tipped his head.

Bri looked in the direction he indicated.

Chase, one hip propped against the wall, sipped champagne from a fluted glass. A stunning redhead in emerald silk stood beside him, her perfectly manicured hand on his arm.

Jealousy, unreasonable and unexpected, hit Bri with all the impact of a rocket launch. What was wrong with her? She couldn't possibly feel anything for this man. She didn't know where he lived, what he did for a living. Heck, she didn't even know his real name.

And then she realized that none of that mattered. He affected her like no one else ever had.

His gaze lifted and met hers. She quit breathing and simply stood where she was. The flow of traffic moved around her, jostled her as people made their way to the hors d'oeuvres.

Eyes never leaving hers, he bent his head and murmured something to the redhead. Then he came back to her. Neither spoke. The silence was intense. Earth shattering. Electric.

Brianna shook her head to clear it. 'Would you like something to eat?'

41

She picked up a plate and wandered along the table, choosing a bit of caviar, some canapés, several pieces of fruit, food she doubted she'd be able to eat.

When she turned, she found her fiancé wrapped in the embrace of a sexy-looking brunette. They stood just far enough away that she couldn't hear their exchanged words over the noise of the crowd.

Brianna watched as the brunette brushed her cheek over Chase's lips and made a kissy-motion in the air. One of those phony gestures society loved, it reminded her of a fish gasping for air.

Then the woman tossed her head back and laughed at something he said.

'Oh!' Brianna plucked a piece of celery from her plate and bit into it, taking out her frustration on the crispy vegetable.

She frowned. Obviously, the two knew each other. It seemed that her Chase had a lot of lady friends.

Her Chase. The toe of Brianna's sparkling red sandal tapped, but not in time to the music. No. It tapped to the tune of her rising temper.

'It doesn't look good,' she muttered around the mouthful of celery. 'He's my fiancé.'

Close to pouting, she caught the sparkle in his green eyes and wished he really was her Chase. But no, it was better this way. No strings attached. No expectations beyond tonight. No disappointments. She had vowed to steer clear of relationships and keep herself out of trouble.

When he finished his conversation, he rejoined her.

Bri swallowed the last of her veggie. 'Beautiful woman.'

'Uh-huh.'

Her eyes narrowed. 'Nice dress.'

'Uh-huh.'

He said no more. Tamping back her temper, she reminded herself that they owed each other no explanations.

Still, she sent a wish fluttering to her fairy godmother. *A few split ends? A zit on the end of her nose? Come on, Godmom, the competition can't be that perfect!*

The night passed in a whirlwind of dance and laughter. Brianna marveled as Chase charmed everyone in the room.

Michael and Lawrence Haines, the company's big guns, loved him. He'd fascinated her friends and associates. There wasn't a female in the vicinity who didn't want to take her place in this man's arms.

Bri caught a glimpse of herself as the two of them danced. A stranger stared back at her. She looked different—beautiful, desirable.

Her fiancé seemed to be everything any woman could want and more. Except permanent.

But, then, she'd decided long ago against

any long-term relationships. Temporary was what she did best. She had two legs of her own and was determined to stand on them. Men provided a false sense of security that led a girl blindly down the primrose path to calamity. She'd learned that lesson well from her father, a master teacher.

But this man, more than most, represented temptation personified. Her fingers itched to muss his hair, loosen his bow tie . . .

Somewhere in the great hall, a clock struck twelve. The end of Cinderella's fantasy.

'Midnight,' she said quietly. 'So soon.'

Clearly, Chase knew the story line, too. He took one last sip of champagne and set his glass on a passing waiter's tray.

'Time for your coach to turn back into a pumpkin, huh?'

With a resigned smile, she nodded. 'And what about you? What do you turn into at midnight?'

His eyes gleamed with amusement. Sliding a finger along her cheek, he whispered, 'A prince, still, of course. The prince doesn't change. Only Cinderella does.'

'Humph. I don't think that's fair. I never did. Sounds pretty unrealistic to me.'

'Most fairy tales are, Brianna. How about one more dance?'

He placed his hand at her waist and led her, not onto the dance floor, but rather through the open French doors into the garden.

The springtime air was cool, filled with the scent of lilacs and hyacinths. Beneath the stars, they danced, alone, to the muted strains of the orchestra. Wrapped in his arms, she wanted the evening to last forever.

She knew it couldn't.

His mouth sought hers in the fragrant darkness. Her lips parted and allowed him entry. Her tongue met his, danced lightly with it.

More. She wanted so much more. Instead, she forced herself to pull away. 'No one's watching. No need for pretenses out here.'

'We'd better go.' His voice was a husky sigh.

She nodded. It was time.

He caught her hand in his as they strolled along the garden path toward the front of the building and their waiting limo.

Chase surprised her when he drew her across the street. 'Come on. Let's take a minute by the river. I love it at night when it reflects the city lights. We have a little time before our chariot reverts to a pumpkin.'

They walked to the water's edge and stood, his arm around her waist. A few peepers along the river bank added their froggy music to the evening. Here and there, fireflies twinkled on and off and lent their magic to the night.

A gentle breeze blew across the water's surface. Brianna shivered. Chase moved in front of her and wrapped her in his arms to block the chill. His hands ran up and down her back as he held her close and warmed her far more than he imagined. She felt fire lick at her toes, her fingers, her heart.

His blond hair caught and reflected the moonlight. He dipped his head and met her lips. This time she didn't pull away. The kiss deepened.

Across the street, the hall's large entry doors opened. Light and the din from the party pierced the night. Voices and laughter moved toward them.

His voice rough, Chase said, 'We'd better go.'

'Yes.'

He put an arm out to stop her when she turned, a teasing glimmer in his eyes. 'We could make a night of it.'

'In your dreams.' She fought to keep her voice light, but knew he'd be in hers tonight.

A roguish grin on his face, he shrugged. 'Nothing ventured . . .'

'. . . nothing gained. Right!' She lowered her voice to a whisper. 'Thank you for a lovely evening, Prince Charming.'

'You're more than welcome.'

Holding hands, they crossed to their limo. When the uniformed driver opened the door, Brianna slid onto the luxurious leather seat.

'To the lady's house, James. She won't go home with me,' Chase said to the chauffeur and then settled in beside her.

The spacious interior suddenly seemed

46

cramped. He didn't stay on his side, but moved toward her until their legs touched, till his hip rested against hers.

Neither spoke. There was nothing left to say. The fairy tale evening had come to an end.

*   *   *

When they arrived at Brianna's, Chase walked her to the door. Hands stuffed into pants pockets, he kissed her lightly on the cheek and walked away into the night.

Behind him, he heard her door open and then close. When he turned around, she was gone.

He placed a hand over his heart. This was the way it had to be. No commitments, no entanglements. He'd witnessed Ross's pain over Jane's loss, been forced to stand by, helpless, while his brother suffered. He refused to open himself to that. His rule of one—one woman, one date—kept him safe.

He'd done his good deed tonight. So why did he feel so empty?

No love equaled no hurt, he reminded himself. Honesty, though, forced him to admit that the flip side of that motto was loneliness.

He slid into the car. 'Take me home.'

A sparkle on the white carpet caught his eye. Reaching down, he picked up the shiny red earring and palmed it. He would have to return it. Just like Cinderella's glass slipper.

CHAPTER FOUR

Monday morning. Brianna dreaded going in to work. What in the world would she tell everyone? How could she explain Chase?

Not his existence. Oh, no. That wasn't the problem anymore. He had been exactly what she'd told everyone. And more. No. Now she had to explain his disappearance. His permanent disappearance. He'd made it very clear that he was hers for the night only, just one magical night.

The elevator door opened, and she stepped out. Silence greeted her. Silence and smiles.

'They're so beautiful,' gushed the mousy blond typist at the front desk.

'Does he have a brother?'

'A twin?'

'A father even?'

Caught off guard, she stared back at the expectant faces of her coworkers. 'Who?'

'Who?' Stella laughed. 'Your gorgeous fiancé, that's who. Wait till you see what's waiting in there for you.'

Frowning, Brianna crossed to her office and pushed open the door. At least two dozen red roses spilled from a crystal vase on her desk. She gasped and buried her face in them, inhaled their scent.

Heart fluttering, she plucked the card out of

48

its holder. Her fingers trembled so badly she could barely open the envelope to read the note enclosed.

To my princess, with many thanks to her fairy godmother. Love and kisses, PC

PC. Prince Charming. Brianna held the card to her breast and closed her eyes.

And then she remembered. None of it meant a thing, not the card, not the flowers. Window-dressing only. And how could she thank a fairy godmother she didn't even know?

But bless him. This was far more than she'd expected, far more than he'd needed to do. He was trying to help her out by continuing the sham they'd started Friday night. He must have guessed how hard today would be for her. A lump rose in her throat. Rather than rescuing her, his thoughtfulness made the reality that much harder to deal with.

She'd lain awake half the night planning what she'd tell everyone today. Another lie. At three this morning, she'd decided on her story: a major lover's spat yesterday had them both rethinking their plans. They'd called off the engagement, at least for the time being.

Her fingertip brushed a rose petal, its softness caressing her skin. Well, no one would believe that tall tale now. Not today.

She guessed she should just thank her lucky stars, or her unknown fairy godmother in this case, that he'd shown up Friday night. He had really saved her bacon.

Then she noticed the newspaper on her desk beside the roses, folded open to a middle page. The society section. There, in living color, smack dab in the center of the page, was a large photo of Chase and her on the dance floor. Chase's face was hidden from the prying eye of the camera. Hers was not, and her expression didn't leave much to the imagination.

They looked like a couple madly in love. Their blond heads touching, fingers entwined, they appeared totally engrossed, oblivious to everything around them.

Beneath the picture a caption stated her name and position in the firm. Either an enthusiastic reporter, or an extremely bored one, had dug up some background info and devoted an entire paragraph to her.

She sat down behind her desk and ran a shaky hand through her hair. The photograph, sharp and focused, held her attention. She stared at the little she could see of Chase. How nice it would have been to have a picture of his face. Then again, maybe not. This fit. Her mysterious, magical date.

Closing her eyes, she relived their shared kisses. Her eyes flew open, and she mentally shook herself. No future existed here with this mystery man.

Nor did she want one. This was exactly the

50

kind of situation she'd fought so hard to avoid.

Still, when she finally went out to pick up her messages, she practically floated on air. Every eye in the place was trained on her. She smiled shyly and didn't say a word.

*   *   *

Two days later, the glow had definitely worn off. The petals on the roses looked as wilted as she felt. Wednesdays typically were killers, and this one proved no different.

She hadn't heard from Chase. Not a word. But then, she hadn't expected to. She wanted nothing more from him, needed nothing more.

Her head ached, and her feet hurt. What she did want was a nice long soak in a tub full of bubbles. She wouldn't get it tonight, though. Wednesdays the family got together. The whole gang congregated at Mom's for dinner.

If she left right now, she'd have time to stop by her place. She could at least change out of her business suit and pumps and into comfortable denims, T-shirt, and sneakers.

Halfway out the door, she heard the phone ring. She hesitated, tempted to ignore it. Who would know?

Her breath came out in a long, resigned sigh. She'd know.

Lawrence Haines's voice on the other end surprised her. She leaned one hip on the edge of her desk and listened.

51

'Your house Saturday evening at seven?' Brianna picked up a pencil and made a notation on her desk blotter.

She felt her face pale at his next words. 'Chase? I'm not sure. He may be busy. I know he has an awful lot going on. Yes, certainly I'll ask him, Lawrence. Yes, I'm sure it's important.'

Propping the phone under her chin, she plucked brittle petals from the dying roses and listened while her boss praised her fiancé— again. Chase had made quite an impression.

'All right. We'll look forward to it. Thank you.'

Sick to her stomach, she dropped the phone onto its cradle. She sank into her chair, folded her arms on her desk, and buried her face in them, muttering to herself.

'Oh, what a tangled web we weave . . .' The Shakespeare quote had never seemed more apt. What was she going to do now?

Although couched as an invitation, Saturday evening's dinner was, in reality, a command performance. She had to be there. With her prince.

*   *   *

Chase inhaled the silence. Five minutes alone. Exactly what the doctor ordered. Leaning back in his chair, he closed his eyes and massaged his temple with the tips of his fingers.

52

When the shrill ring of the phone jarred his solitude, he tried to ignore it. Responsibility made him reach for it.

He was instantly sorry when he heard his brother's voice.

'Hello, Ross.' His shoulders slumped in resignation. 'I figured I'd hear from you before this.'

'Wondered if we were still on for breakfast Friday.'

Chase hesitated. Could he slip in and out of Madge's without Brianna seeing him? Could he withstand the grilling Madge and Ross would put him through? They'd hound him till he satisfied their meddling souls.

Might as well get it over with. 'Sure. I'll meet you there. And bring your wallet. You're buying.'

'Okay. That was the deal.'

Chase winced. 'Yeah, it was.'

'So?'

'What?'

'Come on,' Ross said. 'What happened?'

'I guess you're talking about Friday night?'

'Right the first time.'

'There's not really much to tell.' Chase straightened the blotter on his desk with his free hand.

'Oh, come on! I saw the article in the paper. And the photograph.'

He groaned. Thank God he'd had his face turned when that shot had been taken. With

53

Brianna in his arms, he had totally forgotten about the press, hadn't even considered the possibility of being photographed.

'All right, Ross, all right. She's beautiful, intelligent, everything a man could want, and I had a great time. Satisfied?'

Several seconds of complete silence followed his comments.

'Did you kiss her?'

Chasc snorted. 'What a juvenile question. Grow up, big brother.'

Ross persisted. 'Well, did you?'

'Yeah. So what?' He didn't elaborate. The memory was so intense, he could barely breathe. 'What else do you want to know?'

'When are you going to see her again?'

'Never. That's the way I play the game.'

*   *   *

Panic-stricken, Bri missed second gear and ground her Karmann Ghia into third, chugging jerkily out of the parking lot. At the first red light, she popped the clutch and the little car died.

'Settle down, Bri,' she admonished herself. When she turned the key in the ignition, the car sprang back to life.

Rather than running home to change clothes, she drove straight to her mother's. Maybe her stepsister Allie would have an idea. Maybe some other relative would 'fess up to

54

being her fairy godmother and cough up her prince's real name. She prayed that one of them would know to whom she was engaged. The whole thing suddenly seemed almost ridiculous.

She pulled into the driveway and counted cars. Looked like everyone but Shaylyn had beaten her there. For the hundredth time, she ran through her spiel, trying to concoct a coherent way to explain this mess to her family.

When she walked in, she found everyone on the back patio.

'Brianna.' Her mother welcomed her with a hug and a kiss. 'You look tired, honey.'

'I am. It's been a long day.'

'Well, you just sit right down here, and let me get you a glass of iced tea. I made a cheese ball, too. Your favorite. Uncle Jim's recipe.'

Brianna dropped into one of the wicker loungers and kicked off her shoes. She accepted the glass and held it to her forehead, letting its coolness ease her throbbing head.

'Headache?' Allie, always the concerned physician, questioned her. 'Did you eat lunch?'

'Yes, Doctor. I did.'

Allie, her beautiful long black hair curling around her exotic face, looked relatively casual today in tailored khaki pants and a white silk shirt. Italian leather loafers covered her size-six feet.

'Something's bothering you, isn't it? I can

always tell.' Her mother sat on the arm of Brianna's chair.

'Actually, there is. And I think one of you is behind it.'

She looked at each in turn.

Her mother, Valerie, looked young enough to pass for her older sister. The same blond hair and fair coloring, the same build and bone structure. At fifty-two, her mom looked fifteen years younger. Trim and attractive in navy blue slacks and top, her face wore a concerned expression.

Bernard, her stepfather, lounged on the glider, his feet propped on the coffee table. Six years older than her mother, he carried some extra pounds around his middle, and his thick black hair had begun to thin. Strands of gray at the temples framed his deeply tanned face. Character lines etched into it gave him instant charisma.

Shaylyn swept into the room. She, too, was blond, having inherited their shared mother's coloring. Her eyes, though, were her father's, a deep, rich brown that enhanced her beauty.

'Hi, everybody. Sorry I'm late.'

Wearing faded denims and a yellow sweatshirt, she glowed with youthful happiness and vitality. 'I aced my biology test. Highest grade in the class.' She waved the test paper in the air.

Then she noticed the heavy mood in the room. 'Jeez, what's wrong? Somebody's hamster die or something?'

'No. But after Saturday night, if one of you isn't my fairy godmother, I might well be unemployed.'

'Your fairy godmother?' Shaylyn glanced around the room, obviously hoping someone could fill her in.

Her father shrugged. 'I don't know what she's talking about.'

Another close look at each of her relatives confirmed none of them had hired Chase. She rubbed her hands over her face. 'I was so sure one of you paid that man to escort me last Friday night. But you didn't, did you?'

'A paid escort?' Shock resounded in her mother's voice. 'Brianna, you didn't—'

Exasperated, she cut in. 'No, Mom. I didn't sleep with him. He wasn't that kind of escort. I needed a date, a fiancé, actually. Obviously, none of you looked at Sunday's *Press*.'

'Oh, dear. I'm afraid ours went into the recycling bin and has been picked up.'

Just as well. Brianna didn't need any of them catching the look on her face and reading anything into it.

She took a deep breath and filled her family in on the details.

Over dinner, they plotted the best way to get her out of the scrape she'd found herself in.

Allie laughed. 'You know, we shouldn't really be surprised by this. Remember some of

57

the guys you brought home, Bri? Honestly, everybody else's brothers and sisters dragged home stray cats and dogs. You showed up with guys. Weird ones.'

Brianna smiled ruefully. It was true.

'Do you remember the one that ate nothing but purple food?' Shaylyn asked. 'Eggplant, grapes, juice, red cabbage. Something about being a descendant of royalty.'

Allie laughed. 'Bri's not the only one. How about my guy from Hawaii who wouldn't drive on Tuesdays and Thursdays because his psychic warned him the number twenty would be unlucky. T's the twentieth letter of the alphabet, so—'

'It made sense . . . in a strange way,' argued Brianna.

'Strange being the operative word,' her stepfather pointed out.

'But,' Shaylyn chimed in, 'he rescued Bri's cat from a sugarcane field.'

'And he gave you J.C. for free.' Allie laid down her fork and pushed aside her plate. Her father immediately claimed the last bite of cherry pie on it.

'Aren't we a pathetic bunch?' Allie continued. 'But you ought to see the nurses at the hospital. We've got a doctor on staff that every single gal is after. Honestly, you'd think he walked on water. He's the catch of the day. A few have managed to finagle a date, but that's all they get. One. No repeat performances. Not from the ultra-cool Dr. Mitchell.'

'Oh, yeah? How about you, big sister? Have you fallen for his charms?' Shaylyn started clearing the table.

'Not me. I'm definitely not in the market for a man. Although I do admit to looking twice at this one. For seduction purposes only, though.'

'Alexandra!'

'Mom! Cripes, I'm thirty years old. It's okay. I'm allowed to have a sex life.'

Brianna watched the interchange with relief and figured the heat had shifted from her to Allie.

Not so. Allie, not about to let it drop, turned the conversation right back to her.

'So, tell me about this Prince Charming of yours. What does he look like? What's he do for a living?'

Brianna shook her head. 'I don't know what he does or where he lives. I don't even know his name. He's a great dancer, really good-looking, and fun to be with. He wowed everybody at the company's bash.'

She told her family about the evening she'd spent with him. Minus the earth-shattering kisses, minus the knee-melting caresses. Minus the feelings he stirred in her when he held her close.

When Allie and Shaylyn's gazes met across the table, it was obvious they'd both read between the lines.

'Uh-oh.' In stereo, they expressed their feelings.

'You've done it, haven't you, Brianna?'

'Done what?'

'You've finally found one that makes you tingle.'

'I don't even know him.' She ducked her head to hide the guilty warmth that crept up her face. The indignant tone she'd hoped for wasn't quite there. 'So, what am I going to do?' She swiped at a few pie crumbs on the table. 'My boss invited both of us to dinner on Saturday night.'

Allie lounged against the wall while her sisters cleared the table. Her fingers drummed on the shiny white countertop.

Brianna placed the last of the rinsed silverware in the dishwasher and turned to her. 'You've got an idea.'

'I think you should place a want ad.'

'What?'

'A want ad. Maybe in the personals or in the lost and found section of the newspaper. Your prince might read it and rescue you again.'

'Oh, Allie, that's really farfetched.'

Shaylyn gave a little squeal. 'No, it's not. I like it. Boy, Allie, good thinking! Not at all like you.'

'No, it's not.' Brianna stared at her older sister. Usually a stick-in-the-mud conservative, this idea was totally out of character for her. Unless Allie knew who her date had been. In that case, this would give her an out.

Allie responded to Brianna's quizzical look. 'Oh, no. I know what you're thinking. For the last time, Bri, I don't know who he is. I had nothing to do with setting you up. I'm trying to help, that's all.'

Five minutes later, the girls sat at the kitchen table arguing and giggling. They wrote, scratched out, and rewrote. Finally, it was done—a want ad for a missing prince.

*   *   *

Friday morning, Chase was surprised to find his brother waiting for him. 'Well, what do you know? This makes two weeks in a row.'

Madge jumped up. 'Coffee, Chase?'

At his nod, she sped off, leaving the two brothers alone. Ross folded the newspaper spread on the table, then casually set it down to the right of his silverware. He sipped his coffee.

When Madge returned with a steaming cup, Chase took it with a smile. 'Got your pad ready, Madge? I'm having the biggest breakfast on your menu today. I earned it.'

'Tough duty, huh?' she asked.

'The worst.' His twinkling eyes contradicted his words.

Halfway through their meal, Ross cleared his throat. 'Have you read the paper today?'

'I skimmed the front page and the sports

61

section. Checked the Pirates spring training scores.' He tipped his head at the paper beside his brother's elbow. 'Why?'

Ross's mouth twisted in a grin. 'I think there's a message in there for you.'

A questioning frown was Chase's only response.

'In the classifieds. Under personals.'

Filled with dread, Chase opened the want-ad section, neatly folded the pages back, then creased them. He scanned the page till he found the one his brother had to be talking about.

PRINCE CHARMING, pumpkin has flat. Needs help. Only you can make it right. Must be repaired by Saturday for six P.M. business function. CINDERELLA.

A groan escaped him. She needed another date. He pushed the paper away and shook his head.

'No way.'

'Oh, come on. What can it hurt?'

'Your wallet, for one. You're already on the line for a month's worth of breakfasts.' He tried to keep it light, but one look at his brother and he knew it was futile. 'I'm not doing this, Ross.'

'Why not?' He jabbed at the ad. 'You can't ignore this. She needs you.'

'I don't do return engagements, and I don't

62

want anybody to need me.' Teeth clenched, he glared at his brother.

'You mean, *you* don't want to need anybody.'

'Damn straight.' Chase stood, leaving most of his breakfast untouched. He tossed his napkin onto the table. 'Gotta go.'

With that, he walked out. He knew his brother's eyes followed him, knew Ross would try again.

He berated himself, unable to believe he'd fallen for his brother's dare last week. Damned if he'd back down. He'd carried out his end of the deal.

It was finished. The end.

Crazy, but it had been more difficult to walk away than he'd imagined. The feel of Brianna in his arms as they danced, the tempting taste of her lips, the memory of her silky blond hair dancing in the breeze haunted him.

Taking a deep breath, he tried to put her out of his mind. Should be easy. He'd never had any trouble before.

Okay, maybe once. When he was ten years old, he had been tempted to ask nine-year-old Marissa to the movies a second time. After all, she'd shared her popcorn and let him eat all the chocolate Neccos.

But that was before his rule of one. Before he'd learned from Ross how devastating the loss of love could be.

CHAPTER FIVE

Chase's fingers tapped the steering wheel in time to the music as he waited impatiently for a green light. He cranked up the volume. Pittsburgh's favorite rock station blared out the latest song to top the charts. Just his luck that the group was singing about a beautiful blonde with seductive blue eyes. He squirmed in his seat, a vision of Brianna fogging his mind.

Behind him, a horn honked and jolted him from his reverie. He ground the Jeep into gear and crossed the intersection. Halfway down the block, he spotted a parking space in front of a florist shop and zipped in.

What the heck? What could it hurt? This time, though, he'd be prepared. He'd go into battle in full armor, and this time Brianna wouldn't find any chinks in it.

A little bell tinkled over the shop door. He stopped just inside, hands jammed in his pockets, jingling the coins there. He didn't want anything fancy. Two large stems of iris, nearly the same shade of blue as Brianna's eyes, caught his attention. Perfect.

Chase gave the clerk directions for delivery and paid her. Then he grabbed a card and a pen. The first two attempts ended up in the wastebasket beside the register. He frowned and picked up a third card, determined to get this one right. The pen drummed against his chin as he mentally composed his answer to Brianna's want ad, praying she had indeed placed it.

What if Ross and Madge were wrong? What if someone else had sent her prince a message in the classifieds and he showed up tomorrow night unexpected? Even more important, why did it matter so much that she needed him again?

Pen poised above the card, he finally scrawled a few words.

Cinderella, message received. Will rescue you via my coach at six. Your prince.

Maybe he should sign it 'PC' again. 'Your prince' sounded pretty personal, pretty long-term. Almost . . . possessive. He scowled at the card, then pushed it toward the clerk.

Time to get to work. He was late now. One more thing he could blame on Ross.

*   *   *

Somehow, Brianna made it through the day. Every time the intercom buzzed, she braced herself, certain she'd hear Lawrence's voice on the other end, confirming tomorrow's dinner. Apparently, though, it never crossed his mind that would be necessary. People jumped to do his bidding, and he had no reason to believe she would be any different.

65

Law books cluttered the surface of her desk. The brief she needed for next week's court date remained unfinished. She'd have to work overtime on Monday to wrap it up. A little girl's future hung in the balance. Being a lawyer brought responsibilities that sometimes weighed her down, but made the victories all that much sweeter. And she would win this one! Losing simply wasn't an option where the child in this case was concerned.

Brianna stuffed several files into her briefcase and closed her office for the weekend. She rode the elevator down to the first floor.

The night security guard stood in the lobby, one hand on his holster. He tipped his hat at her.

'Night, Ms. Winters.'

'Good night, Mike. Have a good weekend.'

'You, too, ma'am.'

'Thanks.' Bri sighed. 'I'll try.'

She pushed through the door and stepped out into the balmy spring evening.

With the advent of daylight saving time, it was still light, though her watch showed well past seven. Juggling her briefcase and purse, she shrugged out of her pale yellow suit jacket. The delightful warmth of the air held the promise of summer.

She passed a newspaper vending machine. Curiosity got the better of her. She stopped, dug through her purse for three quarters, and turned back to buy a paper. *Pittsburgh Press* in hand, she crossed the parking lot to her little red Karmann Ghia.

After she tossed her briefcase into the back seat, she opened the sun roof to let in the gentle breeze. Then she surrendered to the temptation she'd fought all day. Turning to the classifieds, she scanned the personal column.

There it was. Her ad. In black and white for all the world to see.

Had anyone at the office guessed?

More important still, had her prince seen it and understood?

How pathetic to be forced to resort to something like this! Placing a want ad for a date! Chagrined, she tossed the paper to the passenger-side floor. It landed on the bag containing this morning's donut wrapper and Styrofoam coffee cup. She grimaced. Time to clean out this car.

Her life—along with her house and her car—was a mess. But not her work. There, she maintained control.

Except today.

Today the charade she had to play had interfered even at the office. Well, no more. Regardless of the outcome of all this, Monday would find her back on track at work.

If she had a job.

But Lawrence couldn't fire her for being a no-show at a social engagement. Could he? She nibbled her bottom lip as she pulled onto the busy street and merged with the heavy after-work traffic.

* * *

Twilight settled over the city during her drive home. For Christmas, Bernard had installed a timer on her porch light. Its glow welcomed her now. Hands filled with the poorly folded newspaper, fast-food bag, purse, and briefcase, Brianna used her knee to nudge the car door shut.

Halfway up her front porch steps, she spotted the long white florist's box that lay in front of her screen door.

'Oh, please, please, fairy godmother, let them be from Chase. Just one more time.' She whispered the words and managed to cross the fingers that clutched her briefcase.

Depositing her armload onto the white wicker chair closest to her, she stopped, nearly sick with anticipation and doubt.

She needed him for a business affair, she reminded herself. Nothing more. Certainly nothing personal.

Under the soft rays of the porch light, she lifted the box to the round wicker table. Setting it down on the blue-and-white checked tablecloth, she held her breath as she slowly removed the top. Two stalks of blue iris lay nestled in tissue paper, perfect in their simplicity. White gardenias, a red rose, and now startlingly blue iris. His taste in flowers ran to the eclectic—if these *had* come from him, she cautioned herself.

She spied a card tucked between the blossoms and sword-shaped leaves and pulled it out. As she read it, relief swept through her. Another emotion nagged at the back of her mind, but she refused to admit even the possibility that she herself wanted more.

Briefly she wondered at his willingness to bail her out, but then pushed that away also, reluctant to dig into any of it too deeply.

However, this finished it, she promised herself. Their second and final date. Maybe together they could arrange a slight crack in their relationship to show toward the end of the evening. That way, Lawrence would buy her 'breakup' story next week. It was time to end this increasingly complicated lie.

In the meantime, she would have one more evening with Chase.

The phone rang as she opened the door. She dashed to it, saw the blink of the red message light. Her heart skipped a beat when she answered.

'Oh, hi, Allie.'

'Gee, don't sound so excited.'

'Sorry. I just got home.'

'And you hoped I was the man of your dreams calling.'

Brianna laughed. 'Actually, I was on the front porch, opening a box of flowers from my prince.'

She looked again at the card in her hand. Bold strokes of black across the stark white envelope spelled out her name. Nothing hesitant in his handwriting. She could read it, though, which put to rest the notion that he might actually be a doctor as she had claimed.

'So?' Her sister's voice cut into her thoughts.

'Soooo . . .' She dragged the word out and then hurried through the rest. 'He'll be here tomorrow night at six.'

Brianna didn't need to check the mirror over her bookcase to know she was flushed and smiling.

'Do you want to borrow the little black dress?'

She laughed. 'No, thanks.'

Last year Allie had wanted to knock the socks off a new beau. The three sisters had shopped together for *the* killer dress, a slinky piece of silk that guaranteed success. The poor guy hadn't known what hit him. Problem was, the creep turned out to be married—with two kids. Rather reminiscent of Brianna's father. He'd only had one child, though. Her.

'You know, Allie, I'm surprised that dress didn't end up in the rag bag.'

'Are you kidding? It's too sensational for that. Nope, I got rid of the guy and kept the dress. Figure I got the better of the two.'

'Well, since we're going to my boss's house,

70

I think I'd better pass. I'll probably wear one of my suits.'

Allie groaned.

'What? This is business. Not a real date.'

'Yeah, yeah, yeah. But promise me. Don't wear a suit.'

'Okay, okay. I'll come up with something.'

'Be sure you do. Catch you later.'

Brianna put the flawless irises in a vase of water. She started to set them on the kitchen table, picked them up, and impulsively carried them into her bedroom. On her dresser, they'd be the last thing she'd see tonight and the first thing she'd see in the morning.

She frowned. What was she doing? She strode into the living room and plunked the vase down on the coffee table. Better.

The blinking red light on her answering machine again caught her eye. She hit the play button.

A flat recorded message sounded. 'This is the *Pittsburgh Press* automated voice-mail service. Press one to hear your voice-mail responses from today's classified. Press two to save your messages till a later time. If you have a rotary phone, please stay on the line.'

'I didn't rent a voice-mail box,' Bri sputtered 'I—'

The automated voice interrupted her. 'You have nine messages.'

The first began automatically.

'Well, hello there, Cinderella,' a strange

71

male voice drawled. 'Don't know about the shoe, but I bet we'll fit together real nice. Know what I mean?' He recited a phone number and told her to call.

The second call turned out to be basically the same, as did the third, fourth, and fifth. By the time she'd listened to bachelor number eight sing his own praises and offer suggestive activities they could perform inside a pumpkin, Bri thanked heaven she hadn't taken the calls in person. Allie and Shaylyn needed to hear these messages before they considered placing any more personal ads. There were a lot of weirdos out there!

The last voice-mail came on. This man had a shoe fetish, so the fairy tale fit right into his fantasies. She hung up.

Lunch a distant memory, her stomach rumbled. Ravenous, she dug through the leftovers in her fridge, finally settling on a melted cheese and tuna sandwich. A cup of tomato soup, along with a glass of cold milk, rounded out her solitary Friday night meal.

Burrowing into the loose pillows on her sofa, Brianna turned on the TV and flipped channels till she found an *I Dream of Jeannie* rerun. She ate while Jeannie outwitted her master's boss. Fitting. Too bad she didn't have a few magic tricks of her own for tomorrow night's dinner with the boss. But she did have her fairy godmother helping out, didn't she? What more could a girl want?

72

She couldn't decide whether her fairy godmother's interference had helped or hurt, though. But the truth was bound to come out sometime. How she and Chase had made it through the first date still mystified her. But to expect to pull it off again? At a small dinner party? She couldn't pretend she had a fiancé any longer. And anyway, he hadn't called to confirm.

An hour and a half later, she'd barely moved. Her dirty dishes sat on the coffee table beside last night's empty tea cup. When a loud yawn escaped her, she stretched, then dug under the cushion for the remote control and switched off the television. Time for bed.

She changed into a worn-out Steelers T-shirt and slipped into bed, luxuriating in the softness of the sheets. A sigh escaped her tired body. It had been a long day.

Her head had barely settled on the pillow when the phone rang. She groaned. Why hadn't she muted the thing? She decided to let it ring, unable to believe anyone would call this late.

With half an ear, she listened as the machine clicked on.

*   *   *

Relief mingled with disappointment as Chase listened to the recorded message. The smooth, sultry voice conjured up memories of the party

73

they'd attended, of Brianna's small, tight body tucked against his on the dance floor, of her lips warm and sweet.

At the tone, he cleared his throat. 'Chase here. I wanted to confirm tomorrow night. Guess—'

'Hello? Chase?' Her voice, soft and sleepy, set him on fire.

'Brianna? Figured you'd be out.' He grimaced. He wasn't fishing! He didn't care what she did on Friday nights. Her real life was none of his business.

'No, actually, I'm in bed.'

He pinched the bridge of his nose and closed his eyes, hoping to block the image her words conjured up. It didn't work. A vision of her, alone in bed, soft and sleepy . . . why fight it?

'Chase? You still there?'

'Yeah.' He dropped to the side of his bed and flopped backward, toeing off his shoes. 'I, ah, thought I'd better check to make sure you got my message. I assume that was your ad.'

The sadness in her deep sigh was audible over the phone.

'Yes, I did, and yes, it was. Lawrence called Wednesday to invite us to his house for dinner. I tried to say no, but . . .'

'Yeah, I know. Been there. A direct order couched as an invitation. One you don't dare turn down.'

'Exactly.'

74

Silence settled between them. He wondered what she was wearing, pictured her lying in that antique bed he'd glimpsed.

At last she said, 'I'm so sorry to ask you to do this again. Believe me, I won't make it a habit.'

'Hey, no problem. We all end up in a bind once in a while.'

He scowled, despite his polite words. What in the hell was he talking about? He'd never in his life been involved in anything as bizarre as this. Fairy godmothers, want-ad dating. Jeez.

'So, um, I don't want to keep you up,' he continued. 'You need me there at six?'

'That would be perfect. I've never been to Lawrence's before, but I have his address. He insists it's easy to find.'

'Okay, well, pleasant dreams, then,' he whispered.

'You, too.' Her words brushed his ear.

He dropped the phone onto the cradle as if it were actually hot and closed his eyes, a provocative image of her burned into them.

Forget the chaos in her living room. Her bedroom, her sanctuary, would be tidy. The same feminine decor would carry through, though. He was sure of that.

The walls, palest yellow, would mirror the color of her hair. A large white bed with a flowered cover would dominate the room. Her lacy sheets would smell fresh and sweet, sexy and hot. They would smell of her.

He felt his body react and ran a hand over his face to stem the current that threatened to sweep him under. His mind rebelled, though, and continued its tour of her room. A candle or two would flicker on the bureau, casting rainbows where light touched crystal perfume bottles . . .

Brianna, herself, would be covered in the sheerest of black lace. No. Make that red lace. Her blond hair would gleam against her signature color. Her skin . . .

He groaned and rolled over, covering his head with the pillow and telling himself sternly to stop thinking about her.

Finally, he fell asleep and dreamed of his Cinderella.

In his dream, they both wore leather, his black, hers fire-engine red. Wisps of golden hair escaped her long, loose ponytail and brushed her face as they sped through darkened streets on his Harley.

Her arms were wrapped around him and she pressed her body against his, holding on for dear life. She dropped kisses, hot and arousing, along the back and side of his neck, nibbled his ear.

A light turned red. He brought the big bike to a stop. It thrummed beneath them. He turned in his seat and drew her to him. Their lips met in a passionate kiss. His hand slid beneath the short leather jacket she wore . . .

Bri drifted off to sleep and dreamed of Chase. Elegant in his tux, he whisked her off to dinner at a fabulous Italian restaurant. In Rome. Via his private jet.

They linked fingers as Luciano Pavarotti serenaded them. Champagne was chilling in a bucket beside the intimate corner table. Fresh flowers provided the centerpiece; the fragrance of roses and lilies surrounded them. Swans drifted lazily on the lake outside the window, their images reflected on moonlit water. Thousands of stars twinkled in the midnight blue sky above, while tall, tapered candles flickered at the table, adding to the evening's romantic ambience.

Several famous models stopped to flirt, but left pouting when Chase claimed none matched the beauty of his Brianna. He turned her hand and dropped sweet kisses in the palm, along the inside of her wrist, up her arm . . .

Sunlight intruded. Waking slowly, she fought it, reluctant to leave her sensual dream. She rolled over, burrowed into her pillow, tried to recapture sleep. J.C. moved to the head of the bed and kneaded a spot for himself. She rubbed the cat's head and smiled. As soft as Chase's hair. How would it feel to wake beside him?

She yawned and stretched, then opened her

eyes. Time to rise and shine. Literally. Every inch of this place would sparkle when her prince arrived tonight.

Thirty minutes later, fueled by a bagel and coffee, she rolled up her sleeves and attacked the windows, polishing them till they glistened. Sunshine fractured into rainbows on their beveled edges and bounced bright spots of color across her living room.

By lunchtime, she'd scrubbed, dusted, vacuumed, and polished her entire house. Satisfied, hands on her hips, she surveyed her small but spotless kingdom. J.C. wound himself around her denim-clad legs and purred up a storm.

'Well, old fellow, what do you think? Quite an improvement, huh?' She leaned down and scratched the cat between his ears. His motor revved up another few notches, the vibration from his purr loud enough to echo in the newly clean and uncluttered room.

A few books still lay piled on the floor. She opened a drawer and stuffed them in. Pushing with her knee, she managed to force it shut.

'Good enough. I'm calling it quits. Come on, J.C. Let's eat.'

She wandered into the kitchen, the old black cat underfoot the entire trip. Brianna opened a can of tuna and made a sandwich for herself before she emptied the rest into her pet's bowl. She let him have tuna only now and then as a rare treat, per the vet's instructions.

'I still can't believe I'm doing this,' she told J.C. 'It's insanity. No way we'll pull it off. There won't be a crowd for us to get lost in tonight.'

Tearing the crust off her bread, she looked at the cat, who ate daintily, ignoring her. She continued talking. 'Maybe I should just 'fess up and be done with it.' She popped a crumb into her mouth. 'Right. That would make about as much sense as jumping off a bridge. The effect would be pretty much the same. Professional rather than physical suicide.'

Nerves got the better of her, and she tossed the rest of her sandwich into the garbage.

'Let's see what I can find to wear—other than a suit.'

In the bedroom she dug through her closet and rejected outfit after outfit. Too blah, too frivolous, too conservative, not conservative enough.

By the time she finally decided on a forest green cotton-knit turtleneck dress, her bedroom was a shambles. Clothes lay strewn and draped over every inch. She groaned.

Well, the closet was due for a spring cleaning. Looked like now might be a good time. Besides, it would give her something to do. She still had four hours till her prince showed up. Plenty of time to get both this room and herself in shape before dinner.

*　　　*　　　*

After trading vehicles with Ross, Chase debated whether or not to pick up flowers. No, he wouldn't.

'This is a business meeting, not a date. I'm her driver. That's it. Period.'

A driver who would eat dinner with her. An impersonator who would pretend to be her fiancé. Impatient for the light to change, he ran sweaty palms down the sides of his dress pants.

Tonight had to be strictly hands-off, and he wasn't going to think about how it looked to Lawrence or anyone else. Forget the window-dressing. Last night's dreams had nearly killed him. After this evening, this blond beauty was out of his life.

He steered Ross's silver Lexus to the curb in front of Bri's small house. An older home, the outside radiated old-fashioned peacefulness. A white porch wrapped around the front, its perimeter bordered by flower beds that would spring into blossom any day now. White wicker provided seating, either for late night star-gazing or early morning coffee. He liked the look of the place even more this time.

Get it over with, he told himself. He bolted from the car and strode purposefully up her walk. Jabbing the doorbell with his index finger, he listened to the chimes ring inside. No more than ten seconds passed before Brianna opened the door.

Rational thought fled. A simple green dress covered her from neck to ankles, yet she stole his breath. All week long, he'd tried to convince himself that their first 'date' had been a fluke, the result of the almost magical circumstances under which they'd met, the fine clothes and sumptuous setting.

Tonight, this moment, negated all his arguments.

She turned to pick up her bag, and he whistled.

With an affronted look, she whirled on him.

Throwing his hands up in the age-old sign of surrender, he said, 'The whistle was for your house.' He tipped his head, studied her. 'Although I have to confess you deserve one hell of a wolf whistle yourself.'

He stepped inside and wandered through her living room. Spic and span, every inch of it. 'What a difference!'

'You caught me on a bad day last time.'

He didn't answer. His raised brows said it all.

She had the grace to blush. 'Okay, okay. I'm no Hannah Homemaker. Guilty as charged.'

'Now you sound like a lawyer.'

'I *am* a lawyer.' She hesitated. 'What are you?'

'Hungry.' He neatly side-stepped her question. 'Ready?'

He stood on the comfortable porch while she locked the house. Then, his hand on the small of her back, they moved down the walk toward his car. She pulled away. Obviously, the lady also meant to keep tonight strictly business. Fine with him. Exactly the way he wanted it.

She slid into the Lexus and ran her hand over the leather upholstery. 'Great car.'

'Yeah, it is. But it's not mine. I traded cars with my brother. Mine's a Jeep. I figured you'd want something a little more dignified, a little more in keeping with my image as a doctor.'

'Actually, I love Jeeps. But thanks. That was very thoughtful of you, Chase.'

He felt his lips curl in a self-mocking smile. 'Yep, that's me. Thoughtfulness personified.'

*   *   *

Brianna was relieved to discover they weren't dining alone with the big chief—three other couples had been invited. She should have realized that would be the case, but unreasonable panic had interfered with logical thought.

The dinner conversation politely skirted anything too personal. She relished the inane talk of people determined to appear friendly while giving away nothing about themselves. The empty chatter of acquaintances rather than friends.

At a lacquered ebony table, dessert in front of her, Brianna sent Chase a grateful smile.

Soon they would be able to escape and end this charade.

He read her thoughts and reached for her hand under the table. The light squeeze, meant to reassure, sent a wave of passion rocketing through her.

Startled, she pulled away from his touch. Her gaze swept his face. The thunderstruck expression there mirrored her own.

Then Lawrence claimed her attention.

'I was telling Stan here, Brianna, what an asset you are to our firm.'

'Oh?'

'Did you read the article the *Press* ran on you?'

Mutely, she nodded. She'd seen it. Remembered the story and picture all too well. Had Chase?

'They like your sincerity, Brianna. Your reputation for doing the right thing.'

She fidgeted in her chair, knowing full well that Chase was aware of it. Unable to face him, she picked at the crust of her caramel almond pie with a fork.

What a joke! Here she sat with Chase beside her posing as her fiancé, the two of them deceiving her boss and fellow workers. Somehow she didn't think she really qualified as a model of sincerity and integrity. Right now she was being about as honest with her boss as her dad had been with his family way back when.

'This case with the little Adams girl is mighty important to the firm.' The media people are keeping close tabs on this one. I'm glad you're handling it for us.'

'You two sure do make a nice-looking couple.' Lawrence looked down the table at Chase and winked, then turned to her. 'Only thing that could be better, would be if you and your fellow here were married.'

She swore she heard a noise from Chase's direction, rather like the sound a trapped animal makes. But she didn't dare look at him.

Although Lawrence seemed oblivious to the discomfort his words caused, she wasn't. She'd have a bruise to remember that comment by, she thought, as Chase's hand gripped hers tightly beneath the table. She winced and withdrew her tender, throbbing fingers.

A look of panic swam in his eyes, sheer and absolute terror.

Her boss hadn't noticed yet, but he would. Her mind searched for a comeback.

'We're in no hurry. Right now, we're enjoying each other's company too much to worry about the future.' Her tongue nearly twisted on the blatant lie. Worried had become her middle name.

She felt sorry for Chase. She'd pulled him into her web of deceit, and now he, too, was wrapped in its sticky threads.

'We still need to work out a few things. You know, the day-to-day decisions. Whose house

84

do we live in? Will our pets get along—his dogs, my cat? What pattern for our dishes . . .' She trailed off. Her nervous reply sounded vacuous even to herself.

'When can we start making kids?'

Chase's words jumpstarted her heart. She dared a glance at him, and he wiggled his brows. Perfect. Everyone at the table laughed at his sly remark, and her tension eased.

Somehow, he always seemed to know just what to say or do. Her hero, coming to her rescue once more.

She stole another look at him. He brushed his lips across the back of her bruised hand.

'Sorry,' he whispered. 'Didn't mean to hurt you. Let me kiss it again and make it better.'

Her racing heart screeched to a halt. This man was just too attractive for her peace of mind.

After dinner, the men drifted onto the patio with their cigars and drinks, eager to escape the confines of the house. Two of the women wore light dresses unsuitable for the chilly spring air, so they opted to stay inside. Bri sat with them. She half-listened to the flow of their conversation. Occasionally she added a comment, but for the most part remained detached.

Her attention strayed outside the French doors and fixed on the blond Adonis—her so-called fiancé—seated so casually, so comfortably on a patio chair, long legs stretched out in front of him.

'What? I'm so sorry.' Bri pulled herself back to the conversation.

Eileen Porter, the wife of one of the firm's senior lawyers, chuckled. 'Can't blame you for not being able to keep your eyes off that young man of yours. He's quite handsome.'

Then she repeated her question. 'I wondered how large a wedding you're planning.'

'I'm . . . I'm not sure,' she stammered. 'We haven't discussed the actual wedding details yet.'

From there, the talk drifted to safer ground as each of the women reminisced about her own special day.

An hour later, Bri and Chase thanked their host and said good-bye to the other departing guests. Safe in the Lexus, Brianna drooped against the seat, nervous and worn out.

'That was awful. I apologize for putting you through that, Chase.'

He started the car. 'Hey, no problem. Your boss is an okay guy. I like him. Don't worry about it.'

She closed her eyes against the emotion rising within her, suddenly feeling weepy-eyed and tearful.

'Why are you so nice about this? I could be getting us both in trouble with all these lies. You must want to throttle me.'

They stopped at a traffic light. She opened

her eyes and met his.

'Not really, Bri. Not really.'

The light turned green, and he guided the car through deserted streets. Neither spoke.

When he pulled to a stop in front of her house, she said, 'Don't get out. I can see myself to the door.'

Then she turned to him, extended her hand, and shook his. 'Thank you so much.'

With that, she practically jumped from the car. She closed the door gently and walked away.

Bri forced herself not to look back. Her awareness of her own vulnerability stopped her cold. There were just too many overwhelming feelings to deal with around this Prince Charming. She would not allow a man into her life. Especially this one. Especially since she *still* didn't know who he really was!

*   *   *

Chase gripped the steering wheel to prevent himself from running after her. A handshake. That pretty well said it all.

The lady was probably right. If he kissed her, damned if he'd still be sitting here. The two of them would have walked into that house of hers, ready, willing, and eager for more.

More.

Damn it. There was the catch. He wanted

more. His fist pounded the steering wheel.

He stared straight ahead, teeth clenched. Well, he'd just have to get over it, wouldn't he? Without another look, he pulled away from Bri's house, away from her.

A chill settled around his heart. The fairy tale had ended. No more Prince Charming. No more Cinderella.

No more dangerous flirtations with pain and hurt.

CHAPTER SIX

'Ouch!'

Bright red blood streaked Brianna's leg, then faded to pale pink when it mixed with the water swirling down her shower drain. She lifted her leg and peered at the damage. A small nick. Nothing fatal, no excuse to cancel. She tossed the slim green razor onto the shower caddy. Enough already.

For the umpteenth time that morning, she wondered why she went through all this. Jeez. Her gynecologist was eighty if he was a day and he'd examined thousands of women. She needed a clean bill of health, not a stamp of approval for personal grooming. Still, the visit made her edgy.

'Talk about a wasted Saturday,' she muttered.

She slid the shower door open and stepped out, swathing herself in a fluffy pink towel that smelled of fabric softener. The cuckoo clock in the hallway chirped the half hour.

On top of everything else, she was running late. She reached into her closet and indiscriminately grabbed a pair of jeans and a white turtleneck. What difference did it make? By the time the doctor actually saw her, she'd sport a paper gown.

Besides, Allie had asked her to stop by afterward. She wanted her to take a look at the garden. Her stepsister's 'Come take a look' always turned into 'Would you give me a hand?' Which meant Bri would end up knee-deep in weeds and fertilizer. The jeans and pullover would be perfect.

No time to fuss with her hair. She brushed it back, then secured it with a maroon scrunchie. A flick of mascara, a touch of blush, and she rushed out the door.

Every year, she scheduled the exam somewhere around her birthday as a gift to herself. She gave a mirthless laugh. Some gift!

Half an hour later, she whipped into a parking space and trekked across the lot to a red brick building. The instant she stepped inside, the universal odors that pervade all medical facilities swamped her. Alcohol wipes, rubber gloves, and the strong scent of disinfectant. Brianna wrinkled her nose and waited for the elevator.

When the door slid open, she stepped in and pressed the fourth-floor button. Strange that she even needed a lift. With all the butterflies in her stomach, she should have been able to float up. Her doctor would probably prescribe high blood pressure medication. Hers had to be through the roof.

The elevator stopped. The door opened. Checking her watch, she took a deep breath and trudged down the hall.

A brass plaque marked the third door. Dr. Kenneth E. Wilson. Gynecology and Obstetrics. She took one last deep breath and entered.

Mrs. Sweet, the receptionist, smiled at her from behind a glass panel. 'Good morning. May I help you?'

Brianna managed a shaky smile and gave her name. 'I have a 10:15 appointment.' She glanced at the wall clock. 'I'm a few minutes late. Sorry.'

'No problem, Ms. Winters. I'm afraid, though, that Dr. Wilson's been called out of town. Family emergency.'

For one heavenly heartbeat, relief flooded through her. A reprieve. Yes!

The receptionist put an abrupt end to her elation. 'Dr. Mitchell is pinch-hitting for him today.' She didn't so much speak the doctor's name as sigh it.

A red flag went up. Where had Bri heard that name? Somebody, not too long ago, mentioned a Dr. Mitchell. But her panic fogged mind refused to cooperate. She couldn't place whom or where.

'Has Dr. Mitchell filled in for Dr. Wilson before?'

'Oh, yes. He's very good,' the receptionist gushed.

Then it hit Bri. Dr. Mitchell of the cute tush. Allie's heartthrob from the hospital. Her own Prince Charming's physique flashed to mind, but she pushed it away.

'Does Dr. Mitchell work at St. Luke's Hospital?'

'Why, yes, he does. Do you know him?'

'No. I think my sister might, though.'

'How nice for her. Well, have a seat, dear, and we'll call you as soon as the doctor's ready.'

She started to slide her glass window shut, then stopped. 'You'll love him!' A faint blush tinted the receptionist's round face.

Great! Just what she needed. A young, handsome doctor. Bri took a seat, prepared for the usual lengthy wait.

She was denied even that small respite. Apparently Dr. Mitchell could actually tell time. The nurse ushered her to a back room and issued the basic blue, stiff, crinkly paper gown.

'The doctor will be right with you. He's finishing up next door.'

The nurse's hand fluttered over her heart.

'Wait'll you see him. What a hunk!'

With that, she backed out and left Brianna alone.

Suddenly ready to cut and run, she drew herself up. She was here. It wouldn't be any easier next week or the week after that. Better to tough it out and be done with it.

Determined to appear calm and composed when this paragon of manhood arrived, she sped into action. Clothes piled haphazardly on the chair, she scrambled into the tissue-thin excuse for a gown. The shoulder ripped.

'Stupid thing.'

She looked closely at the tear. If she was careful and didn't move too much, it should hold. Otherwise, she'd be left swinging in the breeze. Literally.

Pink lace panties slid from the chair where she'd tossed them. Quickly, she swooped them up from the floor, tucked them and her matching pink bra under carelessly folded jeans and covered the whole jumble with her white top.

On bare feet, she turned to face the examination table with waiting stirrups and cold instruments. Ugh. She considered bringing a hairdryer next time to warm everything up, but dismissed the silly thought.

Brianna hopped up on the table's edge. A shredding sound reminded her of the need for caution. She peered at her shoulder. Yep. Only the slimmest strip of blue now held the right side of her gown together.

Before she could decide what to do about it, a knock sounded at the door.

Her pulse skittered.

'May I come in?'

She'd heard that voice before. It sent a shock wave through her body. Then the door opened and an all-too-familiar face peeked around the edge.

If she'd been capable of movement, she'd have attempted a getaway. However, she didn't possess a single working muscle. They'd all melted to jelly.

It couldn't be. It absolutely couldn't be. Not even *her* luck was this bad.

The man of her dreams stood in the doorway. The man who had held her in his arms as if she were a precious flower, who'd suggested they spend the night together. Her Prince Charming.

No way! She could not, would not, lie down and put her feet in those stirrups for him to examine her. The thought of it, of him touching her so intimately, took her breath away and left her speechless.

No breast exam, either! Uh uh! Heat rushed through her, as if the air conditioner had suddenly been turned off.

He stood in the doorway, unmoving, the green of his eyes darkened by his deep green lab coat. Those eyes held shock as great as her own. A stethoscope hung from his neck. One

93

hand gripped her file. The other rested on the doorknob. These same hands had held and caressed her.

It couldn't be. His gaze dropped to the neatly typed name on the folder. Winters. Brianna Winters.

He cursed himself for not taking the time to read her chart or at least ask the nurse who his next patient was before he'd opened the door.

Beads of sweat popped out on his forehead. He'd dreamed of this beautiful creature the last two nights. But never once in those erotic fantasies had *this* scenario surfaced.

He struggled for composure. Professional. It was essential to deal with this in a professional manner.

Then he looked back at Brianna. And nearly groaned. As uncomfortable as this was for him, it must be a thousand times worse for her.

He needed to put her at ease.

Yeah, right.

This was beyond awful! Nothing in medical school or in his practice had prepared him for this. The woman of his dreams, a woman he lusted for, had showed up in his exam room.

He hesitated another second, one hand tensed on the doorknob.

She still hadn't said a word.

His pulse skittering like a wind-up toy, he cleared his throat, stepped the rest of the way into the room, and closed the door behind him.

Big mistake. The small room instantly seemed smaller. And hotter. Damn, it was hot!

He stuck out his hand. 'Brianna. Good to see you again.' His voice cracked like an adolescent's.

She took his hand limply in hers, and they shook as though meeting at a social engagement.

Again, he cleared his throat. 'I think we've both been caught off guard here, but . . .'

She rolled her eyes. 'That's an understatement.'

He laughed and blew out a loud sigh. 'Yeah, isn't it?'

'So, you really are a doctor.'

'Guilty as charged.'

He watched as the pieces clicked into place in her mind. 'I should have known. You played the role too well.'

Her words took him back to Catholic school, back to when one of the nuns had caught him in a lie. He shifted uncomfortably. 'Yeah, well . . . I should have told you.'

Her fingers plucked at the torn gown. 'And your name?'

'Is really Chase. Chase Mitchell.'

'You're kidding!'

'Nope. An uncanny coincidence, huh?'

'An almost unbelievable one.' She narrowed her eyes. 'You work at the hospital with my sister, Allie Montgomery.'

'Dr. Montgomery's your sister?'

'Yep. She's actually my stepsister. Which fits the story so far, doesn't it?' After a short pause, she said, 'I thought maybe the two of you knew each other. Had talked.'

She was obviously fishing. Well, he was going to disappoint her. 'No. I had no idea you were related.'

He inspected the shiny toes of his black wingtips and stuffed his free hand inside the roomy pocket of his lab coat. Then he looked up, his eyes meeting hers. 'I, uh, can't do this examination. Do you mind?'

Brianna shook her head. 'Not at all. This is so weird. But it's not your fault, Chase.'

She pulled the paper drape more securely around her, drawing his attention to the torn gown. The shoulder resisted even that slight movement, and he watched as a few more paper fibers separated. Any second now, the last shred would give way, exposing her right breast. His mouth grew dry.

Apparently she decided it was impossible to hold on to her dignity while dressed in torn paper because, with an exasperated sigh, she wrapped her left arm up across her chest and curled her fingers over the shoulder.

'I'll just reschedule.'

'Brianna . . .'

She held up her hand. 'Don't apologize.'

He tried to hide his infinite relief. Not that he wouldn't like to get this lady naked. But he wanted her naked in his bed, the room filled with candlelight and soft background music. Not here. No way.

Just then, a knock sounded on the door. The nurse stepped in, a cheerful smile on her middle-aged face. She looked from doctor to patient and back to the doctor.

Her smile faltered. 'Is everything all right?'

Chase answered. 'Fine. Everything's fine, Sarah. It turns out, however, that Ms. Winters and I'—he fumbled for the right words—'have met each other socially, and we've decided she might be more comfortable if she comes back when Dr. Wilson's here.'

He ran a finger under the front of his lab coat collar, feeling unbelievably awkward.

Comprehension dawned on the nurse's face. 'Oh.'

That one word said it all. She understood.

'Well, then.' The older woman took over with brusque professionalism. 'Why don't we leave and let you get dressed, Ms. Winters? Stop out front, and Lydia will set you up with a new appointment.'

Mutely, Brianna nodded.

The nurse withdrew from the room. Her crepe-soled shoes squeaked on the tiled floor as she bustled off down the hall.

Chase gazed at Brianna one last time, took in the unnaturally high color on her cheeks, her sparkling blue eyes.

His voice husky, his throat tight, he

somehow managed, 'Good-bye, Brianna.'

With that, he left the room and closed the door softly behind him. Then he leaned weakly against the wall, closed his eyes, and covered his face with her chart.

*   *   *

'Oh, no, Brianna!' Allie hooted, then caught her sister's expression.

'I'm sorry,' she apologized. 'Really.' Then she lost the battle and started to giggle uncontrollably again. 'Oh, my gosh, I know you were horrified, but come on. Admit it. If it had happened to someone else, wouldn't it be the funniest thing you'd ever heard? If it wasn't you, I mean?'

'Obviously, it is, anyway.' Brianna stared at her stepsister, sorry she'd shared the most embarrassing moment of her twenty-nine years.

Then the humor of it hit her, too, and she chuckled.

The two fell back onto their lounge chairs and rolled with laughter till their sides ached. Tears ran unchecked down their cheeks. Gardening would have to wait.

*   *   *

Chase smiled as the pregnant young woman left his office. Thank God Wilson only saw patients till noon on Saturdays. He scribbled a few notations on her chart and laid it on the counter.

'There you go, Mrs. Sweet. All finished.' He leaned around the corner of the nurse's station. ' 'Bye, Sarah. You two are real gems. Tell Wilson I'm going to steal both of you away from him.'

Sarah smiled. 'Careful. We may just let you. Then what would you do?'

He answered with a wink, removed his lab coat, and moved toward the door.

'Brianna Winters rescheduled.'

Her words stopped him dead. He heard her muffled giggle. Try as he might, he couldn't keep from blushing as he turned to the nurse.

She made an obvious attempt to stifle her laughter, but failed. 'I guess you two know each other pretty well, huh?'

He forestalled further questions with his answer.

'We're not seeing each other anymore.' His lips turned up at the corners. 'And you can bet I'll never again walk into an exam room without looking at the chart first.'

He saluted her and left.

Ross had suggested they meet at the gym. Perfect. Maybe he'd use his older brother as a punching bag. The thought made him smile. Yeah. That would feel good. Real good. This whole mess was Ross's fault anyway.

Walking to the gym, he worked up a real

head of steam.

When he came out of the locker room, he found a sweating Ross on the mat, in the middle of warm-ups.

'Hey, Chase. How'd it go today?'

'Fine.'

His tone negated the word, warned his brother that all was not well.

'Problem?'

'Nope.'

'Want to talk about it?'

'Nothing to talk about.'

'Okay. Whatever you say.'

'How 'bout you hold the bag for me while I throw a few punches?'

Halfway into a crunch, Ross studied him. Chase could almost hear him figuring the angles.

Finally, he hopped to his feet. 'Yeah, sure. Why not?'

'Why not, indeed?' Chase landed two light jabs, featherweight taps that barely moved the bag. His third blow packed the force of a hurricane. The bag flew back, taking Ross with it, nearly knocking him off his feet.

'Hey, whoa there, baby brother. What gives?'

His gloved fist came up, poked at Ross's chest. 'If you ever set me up again, so help me God, you'll live to regret it. Lainey will be an orphan.'

Before he said something he'd really regret,

Chase headed for the door. He untied his gloves and tossed them into a corner. 'I'm going for a run.'

Ross's hand on his arm stopped him. 'We need to talk.'

Rounding on him in fury, Chase growled, 'There's nothing to talk about.'

'Oh, yes, there is. And it's a conversation that's long overdue. If you don't have anything to say, that's fine. I'll do the talking, and you can listen. I know that's not your strong suit, but it's time you gave it a shot.' He ignored his brother's black scowl and grabbed two towels from the rack. 'Lefty, Chase and I are leaving for a bit. We'll be back, so don't sell our street clothes.'

'Sure 'nuff, boys.'

Within minutes they sat at one of the battered Formica tables in the twenty-four hour diner downstairs, two steaming mugs of coffee in front of them.

Ross took a tentative sip, then set his chipped white mug on the table. His fingers curled around the handle. 'First, you can tell me what happened today to set you off.'

'You really want to know, Ross? I'll tell you. I walked into an exam room today to do an annual on one of Wilson's patients. Guess who that patient turned out to be?'

Ross had the good sense to remain silent.

'Figure it out yet? If it wasn't for you—' Chase rammed his finger at his brother's chest.

He knew his anger was irrational, but the wall he'd built around his heart had begun to crumble, brick by brick. He'd lost control, and he didn't like it, not one bit. And all because of that damned dare. The one Ross had thrown in his face.

'Brianna. Brianna Winters was the patient.'

Ross choked on his coffee. Chase smacked his back harder than necessary, glad for an excuse to get physical. 'Don't you dare die on me. You got me into this mess.'

Watery-eyed, Ross tried to speak. He croaked, 'You mean, the gorgeous blond lawyer came in for a checkup?'

Chase nodded.

'What'd you do?'

'Nothing. Absolutely nothing. I told her I couldn't do the exam, of course.' He felt the beginning of a smile. 'Damn, I've never been so embarrassed in my life. When she decided to reschedule, I about passed out with relief.'

He started to laugh. 'I felt like a ten-year-old with his first copy of *Playboy*. I didn't know whether to stay or run.'

'I'll bet.' Ross laughed, too.

They sat, companionably drinking their coffee, watching people walk by outside.

Finally, Ross broke the silence. 'You and I still need to talk. I know why you've locked your heart away. It's because of what happened to my wife.'

'Ross, I . . .'

'No.' His brother shook his head. 'We've put this off too long. At first, I couldn't talk about it, then you couldn't seem to. When I lost Jane . . . when she died . . . I felt like someone had ripped the heart out of my chest and cut it up while I watched. It's worse than any pain I ever imagined. It still hits me sometimes, especially late at night.'

Ross was quiet for a long moment.

'But I wouldn't, for the world, have missed a minute of my time with her. What we had was worth all the pain and more.'

'How can you say that?'

'Because I have the memories.' Ross touched his heart. 'Because I have her love. I carry it with me everywhere I go, every minute of every day.'

He looked Chase straight in the eye. 'Waking beside her in the morning, the quiet talks at night while Lainey slept, shared breakfasts. I figure I'm the luckiest man on earth. My marriage to Jane was worth every tear I've shed and then some. And I have Lainey, a living piece of the love we shared.'

Deep conviction shone in his eyes. 'Don't you see? Without love, you have nothing. Without love, life is empty. It's like being locked away in a cage, forced to watch the world go on around you without being able to participate. Loving frees you, Chase, releases you, puts you in touch. Lets you live.'

Skepticism filled him. Ross obviously read it

in his eyes.

'Yes, it can hurt. I won't deny that, and I sure as hell know all about that part of it first-hand. When Jane died, I prayed that God would take me, too. I didn't want to go on without her.

'That's the bad side of love, but it's also what makes it so wonderful, so beautiful. To have someone mean that much to you gives life reason and value.'

The waitress refilled their cups and moved on without a word.

'You're missing out on life's true essence, brother, because of me. And it's wrong.'

He toyed with the gold wedding band he still wore. 'As much as I loved Jane and still do love her, if I ever find another woman I can love even half as much, I'll jump at the chance. And you might have it—right in front of your nose.' Concern clouded his blue eyes. 'Don't throw it away, Chase. Don't lose this chance at happiness out of fear.'

'I'm not afraid,' Chase snarled.

'Oh, yes, you are, little brother. You're scared to death.'

When Chase stared into his coffee cup and made no comment, Ross added, 'You need to give it a shot, and I think Brianna might just be the one. Let go. Let it happen.'

Chase tipped his mug and drained it. 'I'm going for that run. See you later.'

The door slammed behind him.

* * *

'Brianna knows the name of her mystery date,' Allie announced the minute they set foot inside their parents' front door.

A strangled cry of annoyance escaped Bri. She elbowed her sister in the ribs. 'Thanks a bunch, Miss Tattle-tale.'

Her sister grimaced and rubbed her wounded side. 'You're welcome. Very.'

In the kitchen, Allie snatched an olive from the tray and popped it into her mouth.

Her mother promptly smacked her hand. 'Don't do that. Wait till we're ready.'

'I am ready. I'm starved.' She paused. 'Want to know Prince Charming's name?'

Shaylyn charged in from the patio. 'I do.'

'It's none other than the drop-dead gorgeous Dr. Chase Mitchell.'

'His first name really is Chase?'

'Isn't that the doctor you said you'd considered going to bed with, Allie?'

Their mother and sister spoke in unison, their questions falling one on top of the other.

'Yes, and yes. Although, I guess the latter's out now. I can't very well sneak off to bed with a prospective brother-in-law, can I?'

Bri caught her up short. 'You know that won't ever be, Allie. I'll never get married. I'm responsible for myself. That's the way it is, and that's the way I intend it to stay.'

105

She caught the quick look her mother and stepfather exchanged. Sadness marked their faces.

'Honey,' her mother said, 'that was so long ago. I've put it behind me. Why can't you?'

'Mom, I loved Dad so much. But he lied to us. He let us believe everything was fine. It wasn't. First we lost him, then we came within inches of losing the house and everything we had.'

'But we didn't, did we?' Valerie's voice carried strong and firm.

'No, we didn't. If it hadn't been for Bernard, though, we would have.'

'Yes. Our savior.' Her mom linked fingers with her husband. 'What makes you think your Dr. Mitchell is like your father rather than Bernard?'

'He's *not* my Dr. Mitchell.' She took a shaky breath. Fear burned within her. Fear because deep inside, feelings she couldn't name, didn't understand, churned.

'Don't you see,' Mom? That's just it. I don't know. And frankly, I'm not willing to take the chance.'

'I feel sorry for you then, Bri.' Her mother turned away to fuss unnecessarily with her birthday cake.

Brianna stared at her mother's back. She knew she'd hurt her, but she also knew she wouldn't change her mind.

Bernard had barely been able to rescue

them. If he hadn't been such a darned good lawyer, she and her mother would have found themselves on the street, homeless and penniless. She'd sat in the courtroom in awe, held her mother's hand, and watched him plead their case. That day she'd decided she, too, would be a lawyer, that someday, she'd be able to help people like that.

But worse, far worse, were the letters she'd found in the attic. The letters from her father to his girlfriend. The letters she'd never discussed with her mother. The letters that had broken her eighteen-year-old heart and set in concrete her resolve to never let love hurt her.

Not yet out of high school, she'd come to the realization that if she based her happiness on the actions of others, she was doomed to a lifetime of misery. Well, it wouldn't happen. Not to her.

Her mother's words, lightly spoken in an attempt to restore a party atmosphere, cut into her thoughts. 'Well, Bernard, have you done your worst to the steaks, or are you still torturing them?'

'They're ready to come off the grill. Done, I might add, to perfection.'

'Wonderful. Girls, if you'll carry the salads, we'll eat on the patio. It's such a beautiful day.' Without even turning to look at Brianna, she said, 'Get your finger out of the icing, or you get no presents.'

Guiltily, Bri licked the bit of pink that clung to her finger. How did her mother always know? She picked up the potato salad and followed the crew outdoors.

CHAPTER SEVEN

Chase threw an arm over the back of the sofa and closed his eyes. Visions of Brianna floated through his mind. Serious, as she studied her boss's face at dinner. Laughing. Sexy. Brianna in all her moods.

Exactly what was it about her that drew him? What made her different from other women he'd dated? He had no answer.

But one thing he knew for certain. He couldn't see her again. Even though she was a real beaut, this one had to be thrown back. Now. Time to remember his 'catch and release' policy.

Sprawled on the couch, ignoring the Sunday *Pittsburgh Press* strewn over the coffee table and carpet, he accepted that.

Sort of.

His brother's words from yesterday afternoon nagged at him. If Ross could try again, why couldn't he? It killed him to admit that his big brother might be made of tougher stuff than he.

A wet nose intruded into his thoughts. He

opened one eye. The piebald bulldog sat on his rear by the sofa, dewlaps drooping, his big, flat nose stuck in Chase's palm.

'Ready for a walk, Bull? Okay. Let's get your pal.' He whistled for the golden Lab who sat at the window watching a robin nesting in a nearby tree. 'General, get over here. We're leaving.' Chase sprang from the sofa and slipped his feet into a pair of old leather loafers. Then he folded the newspaper and placed it in a neat pile on one side of the coffee table. Both dogs padded at his heels as he carried his coffee cup to the kitchen and rinsed it.

'Okay, guys, ready.'

Halfway to the door, the phone rang. He hesitated. Probably better to answer it. Might be a patient.

A grin split his face when he heard his niece's voice. 'Hey, Lainey, how are you?'

He raised one finger to his dogs, his I'll-just be-a-minute sign, and listened while his niece filled him in on the latest in her young life.

She paused for a breath, then rushed on with her real reason for calling. Her daddy was busy, and she wanted to go to a movie.

'Will you take me, Uncle Chase?'

He thought of the unfinished chores, the paperwork he'd planned to catch up on, then dismissed them. He didn't spend nearly enough time with Lainey. The other stuff could wait.

'A chance to hit the town with my favorite lady? You bet.'

His favorite lady. A high-energy blonde popped into mind.

'When do you need me there? The dogs and I were heading out for their potty break.'

Lainey checked with her dad. The movie didn't start for two hours. He had plenty of time.

While they walkcd, the dogs sniffed every tree, fire hydrant, and post. He remained preoccupied with the problem of Brianna. She haunted him, relentlessly refused to give him peace.

A slow smile crept over his face as he thought of a plan. Maybe one more afternoon with her would satiate his appetite. Even Cinderella's prince had needed to see her again. In fact, he had gone so far as to send out scouts to find her.

Yeah. And then he'd married her. And they'd lived happily ever after.

Chase shuddered and herded the dogs into a run.

*   *   *

Brianna stabbed the trowel into the soil and turned up clods of earth alive with fat, writhing night crawlers. She watched them wriggle back underground, wishing it were possible for her to escape her problems the same way.

110

However, some problems had to be met head on.

Not for the first time, she wondered how her mother had handled her husband's infidelity. How had she dealt with those two letters her father had written but never mailed to another woman? Why had she kept the letters?

Bri dug deep into the warm, black dirt. She sifted through the clumps, readying the ground for the new bulbs and seeds she'd ordered to add to her flower bed.

Her father, so handsome, so warm and generous. So open and honest . . . until he'd broken his marriage vows.

John Samuel Winters had a side she hadn't known about till that summer afternoon in the attic, had been a different person entirely from the one his daughter had loved so wholeheartedly.

As her fingers worked the soil, her mind drifted to Chase. He reminded her of her father. Of all the good things.

But there was the rub.

Chase had the same golden handsomeness and charm. Everyone loved him. The nurses at the hospital drooled over him.

Could a relationship with him last forever? Or would he, too, inevitably cave into temptation, stray into another's arms?

Was he what he seemed or was that simply too good to be true? If her father, the man

111

she'd idolized, hadn't been faithful to her mother, could any man be faithful?

She sank back onto her heels and rubbed the small of her back. The day was too beautiful to ruin with these disturbing thoughts.

Nearly noon, the sun shone warmly. She tipped her face toward it to soak up its rays. Spring. She loved it! Everything woke from winter hibernation and filled the world with new life.

Newly opened daffodils bobbed in the slight breeze and smiled up at her amidst deep purple tulips, pink hyacinths, and white snowdrops. She watched several early bees dip into the buds.

She picked up several bulbs and began placing them in the warm earth, patting the soil around them, tucking them in. Humming, she stopped mid-note, appalled. The tune she'd mindlessly slipped into horrified her. *Someday My Prince Will Come.*

Sheesh! Enough already.

If women waited around for princes to rescue them, to make them whole, there sure would be a lot of wasted lives. A woman couldn't count on a man to provide what she needed. Period. She told herself she'd do well to remember that.

Yes, Dr. Chase Mitchell had kept his end of the bargain. Yes, he had rescued her. Twice. Which was exactly why it was time to cut and run. No sense pushing her luck.

Given enough time, she would have uncovered his fatal flaw. Not for one minute did she doubt it was there. All men, even princes, had at least one. On that she could depend.

Damn him, though, for suggesting at the end of their first date that they might make a night of it. Those words, spoken so quietly at the river, had kept her awake until the sun peeped through her bedroom window—on and off for two long weeks. And when she finally did fall asleep, her dreams . . . She blushed and attacked the soil more vehemently.

The sound of the front doorbell drifted through the screened back porch. Must be Allie or Shaylyn.

'I'm out back,' she called, craning her neck to see around the corner of the house.

Childish laughter reached her ears. She frowned. What in the world? She stood, brushing at her pants. A young girl skipped into view, a wide grin set off by twin dimples. Behind her, looking far better than any man had a right to look, came the good doctor, a matching grin on his face.

Bri's hand instinctively went to her hair. This morning she'd pulled it back into a loose French braid, but tendrils had worked loose and curled around her face. Fresh, black earth covered the knees of her faded denims and smeared her face. She wore no makeup and

113

knew she looked a sight. A far cry from her carefully put-together presentation on their first two dates.

But when she looked into Chase's eyes, she didn't read disillusionment or disappointment there. Dismayed, she caught, instead, a cat-could-eat-the-canary look on his face. Her breath caught. An intensely sensual hunger shone in his eyes. For her. The trowel dropped from her nerveless fingers.

'Hi. My name's Lainey. I'm six, and I'm in kindergarten.' The child held up six fingers, then dropped them to swing her arms back and forth. Two blond pigtails bobbed with the movement. 'Uncle Chase said if I asked really nice, you'd come to the movies with us.'

Surprised, Bri looked from the child back to 'Uncle Chase.'

'I said maybe, Lainey. *Maybe* we could talk her into going with us.'

Lainey's nose wrinkled. 'She's all dirty.'

Brianna laughed at the censure in the little girl's voice. 'Yes, I am. Sorry. I'm not fit to go anywhere, am I?'

'Ah, but I know you clean up real good.' Chase arched a brow at her. 'Real good.'

The reminder of their past times together flooded her memory and brought heat rushing to her cheeks. She blew a strand of hair from her face.

'You know, I'd love to go, but I'm awfully busy. I need to get these in the ground today.'

114

'Why?' His gaze held hers.

'Why?' She parroted his question, suddenly unable to put two coherent thoughts together. Her tongue darted out to wet her lips. She saw his heated gaze follow the movement.

'So her pretty flowers will grow, silly.' Lainey tugged at her uncle's arm, then rolled her blue eyes at Bri. 'Men don't know very much, do they?'

Enchanted, Bri smiled. 'No. They sure don't. Good thing they've got girls around to help them, huh?'

She met Chase's eyes again. The laughter in her own died. God, the man sucked her in and pulled her under with just a look. Too dangerous, by far.

She shook her head, her braid swaying. 'I can't go—'

'Bri, come on,' he urged. 'Step into those glass slippers one more time.'

Lainey's ears perked up. 'Do you have glass slippers? Like Cinderella's?' She clapped her hands together and bounced up and down. 'Can I see them?'

Chase put his hand on his niece's shoulder to hold her earth-bound. 'I was teasing, Lainey. She doesn't really have any. Just a joke.'

Bri remembered their first date and how he'd slid the sandal on her foot, and blushed.

'Oh.' The youngster's lower lip jutted out in a pout.

But she didn't miss a beat. Determined, she returned to pleading her case. 'Come with us, Brinanny. Please.'

Chase wiped a hand over his mouth to hide the grin. 'It's Brianna.' He enunciated the name carefully.

She repeated it. 'Bri . . . an . . . a. Bri . . . anna. That's a pretty name. It's different.'

'Uncle Chase said he'd buy me some popcorn. I'll bet he'll buy you some, too, Brianna.' Her tongue curled around the unfamiliar name. She twisted her sneakered foot into the ground and looked up from beneath lowered lashes. 'I really want you to come.'

Bri tried to resist, but the wistful expression in the child's eyes defeated her. She couldn't disappoint this little charmer. Chase had mentioned two brothers, a sister, and a niece. Was there a mother anywhere in this picture?

'Your daddy lent you out to Uncle Chase today?'

'Yep. He took flowers to my mommy. At the cem'tery. It's really pretty there, but Daddy always gets sad when he goes.'

A jolt of pain stabbed through Brianna. She could relate to this, the sorrow of losing a parent. No matter what she'd learned, she missed her father, ached for him. An overwhelming urge to wrap the little girl in her arms swept through her. Only the dirt that covered her from head to toe kept her from

116

acting on the impulse.

'Oh, honey, I'm sorry.' She held out a compassionate hand, and the child took it.

'It's okay. I don't cry anymore. Mommy's an angel now, and she sits on a big cloud so she can watch me, huh, Uncle Chase?'

Bri turned toward him and instantly wished she hadn't. Raw pain ravaged his face, filled his eyes. Forgetting about the dirt, she took his hand in her other one.

He pulled it away.

His withdrawal should have upset her. Instead, it reinforced the depth of his pain. She, too, had drawn away from those who offered comfort when her dad died.

She studied him for a moment, and thought.

Decision made, she said, 'If you guys can give me fifteen minutes to clean up, I'll make your dynamic duo a threesome for the movies.

'But,' she added cheekily, 'only if you cross your heart and promise to buy popcorn for me, too.'

The mood lightened. Chase smiled. 'Cross my heart.' And he did, marking a big X over his chest with his index finger.

J.C. met them at the back door, tail held high. The old cat basked in the child's unexpected attention, and Bri left them to get acquainted while she scrubbed off the top ten layers of dirt.

When she stepped from the shower, laughter streamed to her from the living room.

Young, childish giggles mixed with deep, masculine belly laughs. The house vibrated with life.

Pausing, she listened and smiled. Then the smile faded as a sense of inevitability settled over her.

Did she really want to spend the rest of her life alone?

*   *   *

Glad she'd taken the time to rebraid her hair, Bri hopped into the front seat of the open Jeep and abandoned herself to the day. It was beautiful! Pennsylvania at its best.

Lainey refused to let her out of sight. At the theater they stood to the side and waited while Chase took out a second mortgage to pay for their popcorn and sodas.

A gray-haired lady, leaning heavily on a cane, hobbled over to them. She bent toward Lainey. 'Hello, sweetheart. You're looking pretty today.'

'Thank you.' Lainey smiled up at the elderly lady and twisted onto the toes of one foot. She clutched Bri's hand in her small one.

'You've got your mama's eyes. Lucky you.' The woman smiled at Bri. 'Spittin' image of you.'

Before Bri could set her straight, the lady hobbled off.

'She thought you were my mommy.'

118

Brianna knelt down in front of Lainey and put her hands on the little girl's shoulders. 'She didn't know, honey.'

'It's okay. I'm glad I'm pretty like you.'

When Bri raised her eyes, her gaze collided with Chase's. He'd heard the entire exchange. Her heart hurt.

Armed with popcorn and sodas, they entered the darkened theater and gave themselves up to the fantasy world of the movies.

*   *   *

'No movie date's complete without pizza.' Chase steered the Jeep into a parking slot outside the tiny Italian restaurant. 'Gotta treat my girls right. It's not often I get out with two beautiful women.'

His words reminded her that never again would she spend a Saturday this perfect. Lainey was an absolute doll. And Uncle Chase. Well . . .

No stranger to the place, he received royal treatment from the instant he stepped through the door. They were soon elbow-deep in pizza that dripped with pepperoni and cheese.

Over his fourth slice, he said, 'I'm going to be gone this weekend.' He laced the fingers of one hand through hers. 'I have a speaking engagement in Chicago.'

Bri looked at him a little suspiciously. Why

119

was he telling her this?

'You don't owe me any explanations.' Her voice was tense and she pulled her hand free. 'We're not accountable to each other.'

'I know that, but . . .' He stopped.

Lainey glanced back and forth between them. 'How come you're mad all of a sudden?'

Bri spoke first. 'We're not, sweetheart. We're just talking.'

The little girl shook her head, her pigtails swinging.

'Uh uh. Uncle Chase did something bad, didn't he?'

'Me?' Chase asked indignantly. 'Maybe Brianna did something wrong.'

Lainey climbed down off her chair and walked to Bri. She leaned forward and planted a pizza-flavored kiss on her lips, then wound her little arms around Bri's neck. 'No, she didn't.'

She whispered into Bri's ear, 'I love you. I love Uncle Chase, too, but he gets kind of grumpy sometimes. Daddy says he needs a girlfriend.'

Bri snorted with laughter, then hugged the pigtailed cherub, pizza sauce and all. She put her finger on the tip of Lainey's nose. 'You, missy, should be an ambassador for the United Nations. We need more peacemakers like you.'

'Okay, but not till I grow up.' Satisfied that she'd settled the dispute, Lainey scooted back to her side of the table. 'Now we can finish eating.'

'Wise beyond her years,' Chase mumbled. 'But why do I feel I took the brunt of that?'

'Because you did. You're a man. You're always at fault.' Bri's smile took the sting from her words.

Then she changed the subject. 'What do you do with your two housemates, Bull and the General, when you're out of town?'

A start of surprise registered on his face. 'You remembered their names?'

'Sure.' She laughed. 'They're your significant others, aren't they?'

He grinned. 'Yeah, they are. I'll probably kennel them this trip. It's only for a couple of days.'

'No!' A cry of dismay escaped her. 'You don't want to put them in cages.'

'Can't be helped. Everybody's busy this weekend.'

'I'm not.' The words flew out before she could stop them. Wishing she could recall them, knowing she couldn't, she chalked it up to her soft heartedness where animals were concerned. 'I can feed and walk them. Honest, it's not that big a deal. In fact, I'd love to. No strings attached.'

She met his eyes, read the questions in them, feared the answers he might read in her own. Was she crazy? Two days at a kennel would be far easier for the dogs than any more contact with Chase would be for her. Yet, she'd offered; she wouldn't renege.

'Are you sure?'

Another chance to escape the obligation. She swallowed, but, against her better judgment, nodded.

'Then you'd better meet the gruesome twosome. You done eating, Lainey?'

'Uh-huh.' The little girl wiped her hands on an already greasy napkin, which only spread the sauce from one spot to another.

'Let's catch your mouth. You've got enough red around it to paint a fire truck.' He dipped the corner of his napkin into a water glass, then used it to clean her mouth and chin. 'Well, look there. Surprise, surprise. There really is a beautiful little girl beneath all that mess.'

She giggled. 'Oh, Uncle Chase, you're kidding me again.' Then she looked at Bri. 'Aren't you going to wipe Brianna's face? I see a spot on her cheek, too.'

Chase leaned toward Bri and studied her face. He moved closer still. Her breath hitched.

'Yep, you're right. Here's a spot.' He cupped her chin in his hand, rubbed gently with his thumb on her cheek. 'And another. And another.' His finger traced a path along her cheekbone.

She went with it, told herself it was easier. Besides, his touch felt so good.

The waitress stopped at their booth.

122

'Anything else?'

'Nope, that'll do us. All we need is our check.'

'Pretty little girl. Looks like both of you. Nice combination.'

Bri blushed. Chase mumbled something under his breath and fidgeted with the shaker of red pepper.

Lainey piped up. 'Do you know my Uncle Chase?'

'Uncle Chase?' The waitress snapped her gum and grinned. 'Whoops. Sorry.'

She dropped their check on the table and picked up the empty plates. 'You have a nice afternoon now.'

'We will,' Lainey answered for them. 'We're going to go visit the doggies.'

*   *   *

One word described his place: immaculate. Bri stepped farther into the sun-splashed living room. Not a single thing was out of place. No frou-frou here. All clean, classic lines, and neutral colors. Beige walls provided a quiet backdrop for the oversized leather sofa and love seat. A round oak table and four matching chairs sat in front of French doors. Floor-to-ceiling windows admitted the brilliant afternoon light and looked out over a fenced-in backyard. The kitchen breakfast bar, topped in copper, showcased streamlined oak cabinets.

Chase opened one of the doors and whistled. 'Hey, guys, come here and say hello to the ladies.'

Two dogs came at a run, one a pudgy English bulldog, the other a sleek golden Lab. Chase knelt, and they laid their noses on his knee.

'Bri, this young man is General George Armstrong Custer.'

The golden Lab raised a paw to her. Delighted, she shook it.

'I see that, unlike your namesake, you've managed to keep your golden locks, General.' She cooed as she rubbed his head. 'You're beautiful.'

Then she turned her attention to the other dog. 'And you, sir, must be Chief Sitting Bull.'

The stocky dog also shook hands with her.

She laughed. 'Such good manners. Glad to see you two finally at peace.'

After Chase showed her around and explained the dogs' schedule to her, he drove her home. She insisted he drop her off before Lainey.

He walked around to her side and opened the Jeep's door. 'Dinner Wednesday night?'

When she started to speak, he laid his finger over her lips.

'You can't refuse, Bri. It's a thank-you from the dogs.'

'Chase . . .'

124

'Nope. If they can't do something for you in return, I'll have to kennel them.'

She scowled at him. 'That's dirty pool.'

'Maybe. We're set for Wednesday, then?'

'Stubborn, aren't you?'

'I can be.'

She nodded. 'Fine, Wednesday.'

When she opened her front door, her normally cozy house seemed empty, somehow lacking. J.C. stretched on the window seat, yawned lazily, then hopped down to rub along her leg. He stopped and sniffed it delicately.

'You smell General and Bull, don't you? Well, come on, and I'll feed you. Then we'll curl up with a good book.'

On the way to the kitchen, she spied a hint of blue beneath the sofa. The ribbon Lainey had lost must have come loose when she'd played with the cat. They'd searched for it, but she suspected J.C. had spirited it away. She picked it up and ran her fingers down its length.

Freedom, space, and the ability to run her own life. Was that enough? Did she really want to be alone? Alone, without the ring of laughter throughout the house? Without the teasing banter, the feeling of connection?

The silence now was oppressive, a sad contrast to Chase and Lainey's merry presence a few hours ago. Bri dropped onto the edge of the sofa and rested her head in her hands, the blue ribbon dangling between her fingers.

She'd been so sure she had everything she wanted, that she was happy. Had she mistaken complacency for happiness? Settled for no downs at the cost of no real ups?

This afternoon . . . the three of them had felt like a real family for just a little while. They'd been playacting, though. It hadn't been real. She shook her head.

The reality of involvement meant dependency on a man. Her mother had fallen into that trap, had allowed her husband to handle all their affairs—and his own, apparently.

No. Bri intended to be responsible for herself. She would not trust any man with her life, her happiness.

But, then, she wasn't worried about just *any* man. She was worried about one special man. Chase.

Could she be falling in love?

Twilight deepened outside her window as she fought the demons within. She considered what she knew of her mother's first marriage, compared that to her second. Marriage didn't have to mean dependency, disappointment.

Because of her father, she'd ruled out the possibility of a family of her own. But did she have to? Had she overreacted?

She made good money. Her law firm compensated her well. Chase certainly had a thriving practice, and his finances seemed well in hand. Money wouldn't be an issue.

Trust? So far, he'd come through every time. He hadn't let her down.

So where was the problem?

She moved into the kitchen to start dinner, her sad mood dissipating. Singing an off-key rendition of a half-remembered tune about getting what you wanted, she accepted that nothing but her own insecurities stood in the way of her relationship with Chase. If she wanted him, she could go for it.

*   *   *

Two-twenty A.M. Bleary-eyed, Bri stared at the small clock on her bedside table. They were back.

She turned her face into her pillow and wept.

It had been six years since the nightmares had plagued her. And now they had returned with a vengeance.

The catalyst—Chase.

Remembered reality crashed down on her, staggered her, reminded her why she'd shied away from him.

J.C., realizing she was awake, hearing her cries, curled up beside her and poked her with his nose. She pulled the sleepy cat closer and stroked him while all the old memories and fears rushed over her.

She hadn't been much older than Lainey. Thrilled that she'd won the election for

Student Council and eager to share the news, she'd hurried home to find that her world had disintegrated. The father she'd adored had died in a car accident with no good-byes. He'd kissed her that morning, promised to help her with her social studies project that evening.

And then he was gone.

The first bad dream had terrorized her that night. With each passing night, they'd escalated till she'd dreaded sundown and bedtime. She lost weight. A little girl of ten with dark circles under her eyes almost every day.

At night, she heard her mother and grandma discussing it all, picked up the fear they'd lose the house she'd grown up in. Listened to the phone calls, her mother's tears, her uncle's threats.

In sleep, reality and dreams mixed with an eerie vividness. Uncle Ned evolved into a grotesque monster who threw them and their belongings into the street where huge black and red cement trucks rumbled, smashing and splintering all they owned. Sometimes the house burned around her and her mother, everything destroyed, while she huddled in a corner and watched.

The only thing worse than the nightly terror was the waking reality of that first year after she'd lost her father. The sound of her mother crying, pleading with creditors on the phone and at the door to extend due dates, even selling her jewelry to put food on the table and pay utility bills.

She'd finally been forced to sell her great-grandmother's beautiful pearls to pay the house taxes. A precious family heirloom had been lost. Because of her father's carelessness.

The nightmares had continued throughout school and into college, long after Bernard had come to their rescue.

And through it all her mother had kept her knowledge of her husband's betrayal hidden, until the day that Bri had found the letters . . .

She sighed. It was all so confusing. Her stomach wrapped itself in knots as she remembered all the times she'd found her mother weeping, prostrate with grief, betrayal, and hopelessness.

Bri had always focused on the financial end. But money, she realized now, had been secondary to the real calamity—the emotional bankruptcy her father's infidelity and death had precipitated.

Financially, Bri knew she'd always be okay. Her situation was not the same as her mother's. She was a professional and would always earn enough to take care of herself. But psychologically, emotionally, she couldn't stand to be betrayed again.

Did she dare trust? Could she open herself to that vulnerability?

The answer flashed immediate and unflinching.

Never.

Rather than risk the nightmare's return, she rose, pulled a document from her briefcase, and wrapped in steely resolve, worked till the sun came up.

CHAPTER EIGHT

Five dresses, four blouses, three skirts, two pant-suits, and a pair of jeans littered the bed. None of them looked right on her. In less than twenty minutes, Chase would knock at her door, and Bri had absolutely nothing to wear.

She held up a short-sleeved red sweater and squinted at her reflection in the mirror. Casual, he'd said. But did that mean Allie's idea of casual, which called for Gucci loafers and tailored silk pants and top; or Shaylyn's college casual, requiring torn jeans and a ratty sweatshirt? Probably somewhere in the middle.

She poked her arms and head through the sweater, tugged it down, then reached for a pair of white jeans.

The doorbell rang.

Her eyes flew to the clock by her bed. He was early.

Panicked, she shimmied into her jeans and stared, horrified, at the chaos she'd created. 'So, fairy godmother, what do I do now?'

No fairy dust flew. No wand appeared to swirl the clothes onto their hangers.

'Hmm. Have you abandoned me?'

Yet when she opened the door, she silently thanked that mystical figure, whoever she was, wherever she was, for sending Chase to her.

'Hi, come on in. I'm almost ready.'

When he stepped into her house, he brought with him the smell of outdoors, a fresh, spring night scent.

His eyes skimmed over her. 'Perfect. You look perfect.'

He bussed her cheek. Lightly. That was all he meant to do. But once he smelled her, tasted her, the single, chaste contact simply whetted his appetite. One arm snaked around her waist and drew her close. His mouth dipped toward hers, held, then lowered. It felt like coming home.

He needed her. She was lovely, intelligent, and caring. She was chocolate chip cookies and romantic evenings.

She was danger.

He pulled away and rubbed the back of his neck.

'Sorry.' He held up his hands, careful not to touch her. 'I said tonight would be hands off, and I meant it. This dinner is a thank-you. That's all. I didn't mean for that to happen.'

'It's okay, Chase.' She smiled. 'Listen, give me another minute, will you? A few last things to do, then we can be off.'

'Sure. No hurry.'

After she disappeared, he moved to the sofa, then looked around. A cyclone he hadn't heard about must have hit the area. The lady's house definitely sported a lived-in look again today. But for all that, it was a home. It held all the little touches.

In comparison, his own house seemed almost sterile. No clutter whatsoever. But he liked it that way; it suited him.

'Okay.' She adjusted an earring as she walked through her bedroom door.

He had a clear shot of the bed, mounded with discarded outfits. A smile touched his lips. 'Trouble deciding what to wear?'

She laughed as a blush raced over her face. 'Guilty. I wasn't quite sure how to dress.'

'You chose well.'

She dipped her head in acknowledgment. 'Thank you.'

He'd sprawled casually on her sofa, one arm thrown behind his head to cushion it. He fought not to react as her eyes traveled the length of him, took his measure in the black denims that hugged his lower body, the black-and-white patterned polo shirt.

Finally she pronounced judgment. 'You look pretty good yourself.' She toyed with a small ruby ring on her pinky. 'Before we go, though, I have a question.'

'Shoot.'

'Why did you show up on my doorstep the

night of the charity ball? I mean, I still don't understand how you knew I needed a date.'

Discomfort didn't begin to describe his reaction, and he knew it showed on his face. This wasn't something he wanted to get into. From her expression, he guessed she wished she could take back the question.

'Never mind. It's not really important. It's just that curiosity killed the cat, you know?'

He struggled for the right tone, decided on light. 'She said she'd tell you.'

'She?' Bri pounced on the pronoun. 'Was it Allie?'

She watched his face for a reaction.

'No. Your fairy godmother was—'

She interrupted him. 'My mother? Not Shaylyn. Certainly not Reeny. She didn't even know about it.'

Never good at subterfuge, he reacted to the mention of her friend. The smallest trace of recognition must have registered on his face.

She jumped on it. 'Reeny? You know Reeny? But how?'

He uncoiled his length from the couch and faced her. It was time to confess. He rested his hands on her shoulders. 'Look, it's no big deal, really. The morning of the dance, you wrote Reeny a letter. Remember?'

'I lost that letter. I never mailed it.'

'I know.' He rubbed his thumb over the pulse at her neck. 'My brother and I meet at Madge's Restaurant every Friday for

133

breakfast.'

'That's right across from our law firm.' Wariness crept into her voice.

He nodded. 'Ross is always late.' That was no lie. He rubbed his hands over her shoulders, down her arms, and took both her hands in his.

'So I was outside waiting for him when you came charging by that morning in such a big hurry. Anyway, a letter slipped out of your notebook when you started across the street.' He stopped. 'How much detail do you want here?'

Her forehead creased in a frown. 'So you read it, then decided to play Prince Charming? Just like that?'

'Well, no.' He fumbled, removed his hands from hers, and walked to the window, determined to come completely clean, yet afraid of what it might cost him. 'My brother dared me.'

The admission dropped between them.

'What did you win?'

Her icy tone warned of impending doom. No doubt her once-warm heart matched her voice.

'Friday breakfasts for a month.'

'I came cheaply, didn't I?'

He turned, fists jammed in his pants pockets. 'Bri, it wasn't like that.'

Her hand shot out, found a sofa pillow, and threw it at him, then another and another. His

134

arm jerked up to ward off the plump, ruffled missiles.

'Damn you, Chase. I thought you were different.' Out of ammunition, the pillow barrage ended. 'I should have known better. When will my heart catch up to my head?'

He recognized the pain that burned in her eyes. A kindred spirit, one also afraid of love and involvement. Why, he wondered? Her torment tore at him. Unsure of his course, he tried to ease it. 'You can depend on me.'

'No, I can't.'

'You already have. Twice.' Conviction fueled his words. 'And I didn't let you down either time.'

Tears welled in her eyes. 'Only because you were doing it on a dare. It wasn't me you wanted. Not me.'

'Come on, Brianna, that's not true. You're blowing this all out of proportion.'

'Am I?' Eyes narrowed, she pointed her finger at him. 'I specifically asked if someone paid you to take me to that dance. You said no. You lied to me. I can't forgive that.'

'I didn't lie.'

He took a step toward her.

'Don't touch me.' She extended her arms, palms out to stop him. 'You dated me on a dare. I do hope winning was worth it.'

Frustrated, he cursed softly.

Chin tipped defiantly, she said, 'Well, the engagement's off.'

That stopped him cold. 'What engagement? Ours?' He planted his fists on the sofa's back. 'You can't call it off.'

He took two more steps toward her. 'How can you call it off? It never existed. It was pretend.'

'Exactly. A farce, a sham. Like our entire relationship.'

He rubbed his hands over his face. This male versus female stuff drove him nuts! He'd been smart to avoid it all, to stay clear of emotional entanglement.

Till now.

And she was rejecting him.

Panic nipped at his heart. 'You can't do this. It's not the way the story goes.'

'What story?'

'*Cinderella*. She loves her prince; she needs him. He means more than anything else in the world to her, regardless of the problems in their way. She'd do anything for him.'

Bri snorted. 'Not in this century, buddy.'

'Fine.'

She remained silent, arms crossed defensively over her chest.

Finally, he said, 'Guess it's time for me to leave.'

'Bingo.'

He thought he heard a tiny waver in her voice, but then he noticed the set of her jaw.

Perplexed, he stared at her. He hadn't done anything *that* bad. 'You're overreacting, Bri.'

136

'Go away. I need to think.'

His first impulse was to storm out, to slam the door behind him. Instead, he closed it gently, winced as the latch caught, signifying the end. The end of his role as the prince come to save the beautiful damsel in distress. The end of his time with Brianna.

Depression tugged at him, heavy as an anchor, as he walked to his Jeep. Things had gotten out of hand, escalated too quickly. But he'd never planned to carry it this far, so maybe it had worked out for the best.

He slapped the top of his vehicle. Damn! Who was he kidding? It was already too late. He rubbed his chest. It hurt. He didn't know how or when it had happened, but the seductive blond sprite had crept into his heart.

And just like Humpty Dumpty, he'd taken the fall.

Now would come the pain, the pain he'd worked so hard to avoid. The pain he wanted no part of.

He'd screwed up, left himself open to love. And lost.

*　　*　　*

By one o'clock, the hospital cafeteria swarmed with employees and visitors. Intent on grabbing a fast lunch, each jockeyed for a place in line. The scene reminded Chase of football scrimmages during his college days.

He dug money out of his pocket and paid for the meal. The gray, congealed glob of meat loaf stared up at him. The blue plate heart attack special. He didn't figure he'd have to eat it. Being in the vicinity of the culinary atrocity should be enough to clog his arteries or at least give him heartburn.

Then he spotted Dr. Alexandra Montgomery alone at a corner table, engrossed in a book. Exactly the lady he'd come to find.

He'd spent a miserable night, restless and prowling. Sunrise found him wide awake on his living room sofa, watching a rerun of *Green Acres* on the Nickelodeon channel.

Bri mystified him. Maybe her stepsister could shed some light.

He made his way to her table and glanced at her food choice. A green salad and some fruit. Far healthier than the stuff on his mustard yellow plastic tray, it also looked much more appetizing.

'Mind if I join you?'

She closed her paperback and set it aside. 'No,' she answered drolly, 'but I'll probably have to hire a bodyguard afterward.'

Confusion knitted his brows; then he raised his head to follow her gaze. Half the occupants of the cafeteria, the female half, eyed them. He grinned self-consciously and slid into the seat opposite her.

Alexandra Montgomery. Stunning, yet so

different from Bri. The doctor's dark brown hair curled past her shoulders and highlighted eyes the color of dark coffee. Her jawline was oval, not square like Bri's. But then, they were stepsisters.

He extended his hand and introduced himself.

'Oh, I know who you are, Dr. Chase Mitchell. I doubt there's a woman on staff who doesn't recognize you.' She paused. 'Bri told me you subbed for Dr. Wilson last week.' All innocence, she took a sip of her milk.

For the life of him, he couldn't fight back the groan. 'She told you about that?'

Then he caught the smile that played across the beautiful brunette's face. He threw back his head and laughed, long and loud. 'God, it was awful.'

Allie laughed with him. 'That's what she said. So . . . what brings you to share lunch with me—a medical problem or something more personal? If I had to guess, I'd say it has something to do with my little sister.'

'Dr. Montgomery, I need your help.'

'Call me Allie.' She grinned. 'You know, you look every bit as miserable as Bri.'

He perked up, immediately feeling better. 'She's miserable?'

'Yep. I stopped by this morning, and she looked awful, like she'd been run over by a train. Obviously, she didn't sleep last night.'

She planted her elbows on the table and

leaned closer to him. 'Seems you didn't either. An elephant could pack for a week in those bags under your eyes.'

'That bad, huh?'

'Yep. Trouble with Bri?'

'Heaven help me, but I think I might love her.' Again, he rubbed the ache in the area of his heart.

'You're serious.' Allie spoke quietly, her dark brows knitted in consternation while she studied his face.

He nodded.

'Oh, boy. Heaven help you is right.' Allie laid down her fork, all signs of levity gone. 'Have you told her?'

He grimaced and shook his head.

'Has Brianna talked to you at all about her childhood? About her father?'

'Only that he died when she was young.' His stomach clenched. Her father. The key to her anger, her hope that he was different? Had her dad been a gambler, abused her? Scenario after scenario played through Chase's mind.

'Are you in a hurry?'

'No.'

Allie wrinkled her nose at the food he pushed around his plate. 'Get rid of that stuff. Toss it. It's better off in the trash than in your body.'

'No argument there.' He headed for the nearest receptacle and dumped his tray.

'Let's grab a cup of coffee and go outside to

the garden. We need to talk. Might as well catch some rays while we do.'

The two found a bench. Chase confessed everything, the dropped letter, the dare, and the disagreement that erupted when he'd told Bri about it.

'What a mess. You played right into her worst nightmare.'

Allie shared what she could of her stepsister's background, her problems, and insecurities without betraying any trusts. 'Bri believed and still does on some subconscious level, I think, that her dad died and left her because she was somehow lacking, that he didn't love her enough. Her self-esteem took a real blow. There were some other problems that Bri herself has to tell you about.

'Now you come along. She starts to like you, to think of you as her Prince Charming, only to find out someone paid you, even if only in ham and eggs, to take her out.' The wry look she leveled at him made him wince. 'Starting to get the picture?'

He nodded, understanding all too well.

'You know she'd kill me if she found out I told you all this, don't you? Slowly and painfully.'

'Our secret, I promise.' He crossed his heart and hoped to die.

Allie laughed. 'That should do. Anyway, Bri decided long ago that she'd never fall in love. And then you came along . . .'

She caught her hair up in one hand and swept it off her neck. 'This goes way back. When Bri's dad died, part of her did, too. She adored him, but he made no provisions for them, left no insurance, only a mountain of debt. Her childhood, her innocence, died with him.

'To make it worse, an uncle claimed inheritance rights and tried to take what little was left. At one point, they actually packed, a day away from eviction. Good old Uncle Ned planned to move them out and himself in.'

Chase thought of Lainey. How could any man do that to his niece? Aloud, he asked, 'What would make him think he held rights above and beyond the widow and surviving child?'

Allie grimaced. 'An old will. One that should have been voided when John and Valerie married. I'm kind of fuzzy on the details, but it was a really sticky legal tangle.'

He hurt for the young Bri, for the disillusionment and pain she'd suffered. Her hurts had become his; he was in serious trouble.

Allie leaned down, picked a blade of tender new grass, and twirled it between her fingers. 'That's when my dad stepped in. He's a lawyer. He and Bri's father had been friends since high school. Dad managed to cut through the red tape so they could keep their home.'

'And along the way her mom and your dad

got together?'

'Yep.' She sipped her coffee. 'Dad had been a widower for two years. They fell in love. It's been a good marriage, and they've made a wonderful home for us three girls, his, hers, and theirs. And believe me, we've all been treated the same. There was no playing favorites.'

'You love them.'

'You bet I do.'

He reached out, laid a hand over hers. 'How old were you when your mother died, Allie?'

She looked startled by the unexpected question. 'Seven.'

'Do you miss her?' Chase asked the question for both himself and Lainey.

'Sometimes, yes. But it doesn't hurt anymore. It's hard to explain. My memories of her are blurred. The pain is gone, so only the good remains. I loved her, but I love Valerie, too. I call her Mom. I didn't at first, and being the smart lady she is, she never pushed.

'When Shaylyn came along, it seemed the natural thing to do. We became a family. I've been lucky to have the love of two mothers.' Her eyes shone unnaturally bright with a faint mist of tears.

'Bri loves my father, but it's different with her because the circumstances were different. Then a few years ago, the hurt was compounded by a new discovery she made that I really can't go into. Bottom line, she's never gotten over the hurt her father's death caused. He died in an accident, very suddenly. No time for good-byes. A lot left unsaid and undone.'

'And the bet between Ross and me played right into those old insecurities of hers, didn't it?' Chase already knew the answer to his question.

Allie nodded. 'Bri's so beautiful, so talented and intelligent. Yet she can't accept that someone could love her for herself, can't believe that if she gives her love, the person will stay with her, not abandon or betray her. Old hurts die hard. It's going to be difficult to convince her you were interested in her—not in winning the dare, not just a good time. And that you're in this for the long haul.'

The long haul. Fear raced through him at the words, but his newfound resolve banished it. He said, 'Yeah, no kidding. Looks like we're both afraid to find love for fear of losing it.'

The admission came reluctantly.

He crushed his empty styrofoam cup and tossed it into a trash can. 'Well, I've never wanted a woman this much before. In fact, I've gone out of my way to avoid involvement.'

Allie stopped him. 'Tell me something I don't know. You're a legend in this hospital, Chase. "One-Date Mitchell." Fortunes have been made and lost on the bets placed around here. Which woman could snare a second date with you.'

She grew serious. 'No one has. That's why,

144

when Bri told me about you, I found it hard to believe we were talking about the same guy.'

Her hand squeezed his. 'I wish you well, Dr. Mitchell. But I'm warning you. You hurt my sister, and you'll have the whole clan after you.'

'I won't hurt her. Not intentionally.'

'You already have.'

He sighed. 'It was important to be honest with her. Nothing good comes from deceit, and our whole relationship had been built on lies and half-truths. I figured the time had come to end the deceptions, to come clean.'

She met his gaze, her eyes intent. 'Brianna's in court today.' With a twist of her wrist, she checked the time. 'If you hurry, you can catch her there.'

'Thanks.' Chase stood, then leaned down to drop a kiss on her cheek. 'You won't regret this. Promise.'

Allie sighed as he turned to walk away. 'Ah, what might have been. Great butt!'

He grinned. 'You like my butt?'

'One of the best I've ever seen.'

'Huh! I knew it.' He punched the air. 'It *is* better than average. Guess old Madge doesn't know everything after all.'

'Madge?'

'Long story.'

*   *   *

145

Overhead, sluggish fans churned the oppressive silence. The heavy oak door closed quietly behind him, and he slid onto the worn wooden bench.

Brianna stood in front of the witness stand, her back to him. Today, she'd swept her blond hair up into a twist which showed off her long, slender neck. Dressed in a slim navy blue suit, she looked efficient and professional, and her rounded hips and shapely legs only enhanced the effect: It might not have been her intent, but she also looked sexy as hell, the sexiest lawyer he'd ever known.

She hadn't seen him come in. He was glad. It provided the chance to watch her work, unobserved.

A child custody case made up Bri's schedule on today's docket. A young girl's father stood accused of abuse. After watching Bri and Lainey together on Saturday, Chase had a pretty good idea of the emotional involvement on Bri's part. Add in her feelings about her father and the stakes escalated. She could not afford to lose this case—either professionally or personally.

The court proceedings captivated him.

In a brisk, no-nonsense voice, Bri threw a question at the accused seated on the witness stand. The jurors waited while the man looked at his hands, his feet, a spot on the wall. Anywhere but at them or the lady lawyer.

Finally, in halting sentences, he spoke, his

words an obvious effort to rationalize his mistreatment of his daughter.

When he finished, Bri indicated she had no further questions. The judge dismissed the witness and final arguments began.

Chase watched Brianna calmly rise to her feet and move to stand in front of the jury box. Resting her hands on the rail, she addressed them.

'Ladies and gentlemen of the jury, you've seen the pictures. You've seen firsthand the scars on the body of this eight-year-old child.' She indicated the thin girl who sat round-eyed, her tiny hands balled into white-knuckled fists on the table.

Chase listened, enthralled, as an impassioned Bri went for the jugular.

'Many of you have children. Some of you have grandchildren.' She walked across the front of the courtroom to the table where her young client sat. She pulled the girl's limp, dull hair back to reveal several cigarette burns.

'These are not marks of love. Rather, they are marks of depravity, marks of intentional cruelty. They represent scars, both emotional and physical, that will last a lifetime.'

Bri spoke with slow deliberation, looked at each juror in turn, met each one's gaze squarely. Her voice never wavered; her conviction rang true. She pointed at the defendant.

'This is not a man who loves his child. This

is not a man who wants the best for his daughter. Biologically creating life does not make one a father.'

She continued to drive home her points, methodically, one by one, each building on the last, till several members of the jury wiped tears from their eyes.

Chase sat mesmerized, caught up in the story she wove.

'You must allow Jannclle Adams a chance to live, a chance to grow up free from fear.' She pointed an accusing finger at the defendant. 'Free from the reach of this man. Give her the same chance in life you want for your children and their children. When you step into that jury room, vote to remove her from his grasp. Take away his power to hurt her. You have no other choice.'

She took her seat.

The defense attorney waited a moment, shuffled a few papers, then walked to the jury box, looked long and searchingly at each member. The courtroom fell silent.

He cleared his throat and began. He presented his client as a hardworking man, a father who had high standards for his daughter, enforcing her best behavior, but only because he wanted the best for her.

The attorney met cold stares, received no encouragement. The jurors' body language spoke of contempt and disillusionment. His concluding statements limped to an end, and he returned to his seat.

Chase's heart swelled. He wanted to shout, 'Way to go!' Bri had won. He knew it! Instead, he sat quietly and listened while the judge read the jury their directions and then sent them to deliberate.

Chase watched Brianna shed her professional demeanor. She leaned down to the little girl, hugged her, and smoothed her hair, kissed her forehead. He couldn't hear the words they exchanged but saw the smile that lit the child's features. One more hug and the girl left the room with a matronly-looking policewoman.

Bri arranged some papers, placed them in her briefcase, then clicked the latch. Chase held his breath.

She turned. When she saw him, her eyes mirrored his uncertainty. She stopped as if paralyzed. Time hung suspended.

For a moment, he thought she might come to him. Then, head high, she walked on past, neither hesitating nor acknowledging his presence in any way. Completely and unequivocally, he had been dismissed. She'd made him invisible. And it hurt like hell.

Far worse was the knowledge that he had brought it on himself. He'd caused her pain, his sweet, vulnerable Bri.

He jumped to his feet and caught the heavy door as it swung shut. Driven, he followed her into the hallway.

'We have to talk.'

She whirled to face him. Fresh from battle, her eyes burned fiercely with the fight she'd just waged in the courtroom. Deeper, they smoldered with the pain she and her young client shared. Far worse, they overflowed with the knowledge of his betrayal.

Before he could react, she fled into the women's washroom.

For a full sixty seconds he stood, his palm on the door, and debated whether or not to follow her.

With a resigned shake of his head, he conceded defeat. Temporarily.

He'd wait. Sooner or later, she'd come out, and when she did, he'd be right here. A hard bench propped against the far wall looked like as good a place as any to regroup.

He dropped onto it and tried to make sense of the situation. Brianna Winters was not only beautiful, but incredibly competent, unbelievably skillful at her work. Even before he saw her in action, he had known she would be.

The lady was perfection.

Then he thought of her house and smiled wryly. Perfection might be a little strong. But he loved her all the more for her imperfections.

He caught himself.

Loved. Had he actually used that word? The thought scared the hell out of him.

Nearly half an hour later, the bathroom door opened, and she stepped out. Her red-rimmed eyes widened at the sight of him.

'Bri . . .'

Her cheeks streaked with the tracks of tears, she said, 'I thought you'd gone.' Her voice broke. 'You should have.'

Without another word, she turned and walked away.

CHAPTER NINE

Bri hit the off button and tossed the remote onto the coffee table. Her mind refused to follow a single one of the sitcoms that paraded across the television screen.

The jury had returned their verdict first thing this morning. A unanimous decision. Guilty. Little Jannelle would have her fresh start. Bri mouthed another prayer of thanks.

She should be happy. Instead, she was utterly miserable.

A cup of hot tea. That's what she needed. Maybe some ice cream, too, swimming in hot fudge. Might as well wallow in her sorrow.

Chase hadn't called.

But, then, why should he? He'd waited half an hour yesterday outside the women's room. For what? So she could walk away from him? Refuse to give him the time of day? Why hadn't she sat down on that time-worn courthouse bench and talked with him?

His heart had been in his eyes. Devastation clouded them. But she'd ignored his hurt, listened only to the clamor of her own fears, focused on her own foibles and weaknesses.

Right now, he would be packing for his trip. The last three weekends he'd come for her, spent time with her. This weekend would be different. He wouldn't come, wouldn't even be in Pittsburgh.

She missed him.

She'd get over it.

Wouldn't she?

Halfway to the kitchen, heart set on drowning her blues in a thousand calories' worth of chocolate sauce, she nearly jumped out of her skin when the phone rang. Her heart rate accelerated to warp speed.

Chase! Did he miss her, too? Was he calling to tell her again that he was sorry? That he'd see her when he came back? Better yet, that he'd be over tonight to share another kiss before he left, a kiss that might save her from starvation? Because no doubt about it. She was starving for his kiss, his touch. No amount of chocolate would substitute.

Her hand trembled on the receiver. Gulping in air to steady herself, she brought the phone to her ear.

'Hello?' Her breathless voice was barely audible.

'Brianna?'

The childish voice made Bri smile sadly. Disappointment, hot and piercing, gave way to a measure of relief. Defenseless against Chase, she could enjoy this call, depending on what his niece wanted.

'Hi, Lainey.' She forced cheer into her voice. 'What are you up to tonight?'

'I got new shoes. Shiny black ones. Daddy bought them for me today. They're for school, though, so I can't wear them to play in. 'Cause I might forget to walk around the water puddles.' She giggled. 'I do that sometimes. Uncle Chase says it's 'cause I'm part fish. He calls me his little guppy.'

The child's innocent words pierced Bri's heart. Uncle Chase.

Without coming up for air, Lainey chattered on. 'I called him, but he says he has to go away in the morning, to a con . . .'

'A conference,' Bri supplied.

'Uh-huh. A conference. So we can't go to a movie tomorrow. I'm sorry.'

Touched by the youngster's heartfelt apology and her own melancholy, Bri blinked back a tear. 'Me, too, Lainey. Me, too.'

'Maybe next Saturday we can go. And we can get more popcorn.'

'Ah, spoken like a woman after my own heart. With lots of butter.'

'Yeah.' The giggle came over the phone line again. 'Daddy wants to talk to you. I'll go get

153

him.'

Before Bri could respond, a loud thump sounded in her ear as the phone receiver dropped and apparently hit the floor or a table. In the background, she heard Sesame Street music, then the little girl's shout for her daddy.

A deep male voice spoke her name.

She lost his first few words as her heart stuttered. Lainey's father sounded so much like his younger brother, it made her weak in the knees. And yet, she heard differences. Small differences. She forced herself to pay attention to his words.

'. . . Ross Mitchell. We haven't met, but I've heard a lot about you. Both from this precocious daughter of mine and from my pigheaded brother. I owe you an apology.'

'No, Ross, you . . .'

'Yes, I do. I'm somewhat responsible for this whole mess, so please let me talk.'

She heard his sigh and recognized how difficult this must be for him. Pride obviously ran in the family.

'Look. You and Chase are fighting and it's my fault.'

'We're not fighting.'

'Yes, you are.'

Speechless at his presumptuousness, she kept her mouth shut.

'Chase walked into Madge's Restaurant three weeks ago preoccupied with you. Hell, he all but drooled and started to talk about Cinderella and princes and balls. He practically broke my hand when I tried to read your letter.'

He paused, then admitted, 'I never have been able to let well enough alone. Can't keep from goading him, so I dared him to take you to that office gala. Made the bet you're so sore about.'

She cut in. 'I appreciate what you're trying to do, but it doesn't matter. It's over between Chase and me. Heck, it never really started. Our first two dates were fakes, both of us pretending to be something we weren't. I guess we got caught up in it for a little while.' Then she mumbled, 'Though I still can't figure why everybody believed us. Two total strangers pretending to be an engaged couple.'

She pushed her hair back from her forehead. 'There's no way we could ever make it work. A relationship, I mean. Even if we wanted to. Which we don't.'

Smooth delivery, she thought sarcastically as she stumbled over her words. Her glib lawyer's tongue must have stayed behind at the office today.

'Brianna, I know better than that.' Ross spoke so softly, so candidly, that she had no response. 'The act works because the spark between the two of you is real.'

Silence stretched between them. Then he asked, 'Did Chase tell you about Jane,

Lainey's mom, my wife?'

His change of subject caught her off guard. 'Only that she died.'

'Well, if you've got a minute, I'd like to tell you a story.'

She dropped into a wicker chair and curled her feet beneath her. Phone tucked under one ear, she listened teary-eyed as Ross poured out his feelings for the wife he'd lost, talked about their life together, the joy they'd felt at creating a new little person from their love. Her diagnosis of breast cancer.

A haunting sadness crept into his voice. 'The lump was small. Yet within months, it stole my vibrant, beautiful Jane from me.'

Voice strained, he fought to continue. 'I couldn't have made it without Chase. Through it all, he stayed right there. He pitched in and did whatever needed to be done, whether it was grocery shopping or staying overnight with the baby. He sat at the hospital with Jane and held her hand when I couldn't.

'I think in some ways he took the loss worse than I did. I lost my wife, my lover, my best friend, my child's mother. It devastated me, rocked the foundation of my world. But because he shouldered so much, absorbed so much of my hurt, he hasn't recovered. Chase suffered her loss as well as my pain. It was too much for him.'

'And so to protect himself from any more hurt,' Brianna said softly, 'he steers clear of love.'

'Exactly,' Ross agreed. 'He helped me put my life and my heart back together, but he ignored himself, his own feelings. Now, he refuses to get involved, figuring love's a package deal. That it comes complete with heartache. He's focused on the suffering Jane and I went through at the end, while I remember the good times we shared.'

Silence ensued.

He lowered his voice. 'Brianna, my brother's hurting—because of my meddling. After everything he's done for me, I've screwed up things for him. For the first time in his life, he's fallen, and he's fallen hard. Now, you refuse to see him, and it's my fault.'

She didn't answer, didn't know what to say.

'He'd whip my butt from here till next Friday if he knew I'd told you all this, but I think you have the right to know.'

She still didn't say anything.

'So, anyway, I figure right now you've got a problem.'

She blinked. 'Me?'

'Seems you promised my little brother you'd dog-sit for him this weekend. I'd guess with everything that's happened, that's the last thing you want to do. With a little juggling, I can rearrange my schedule. I'll feed and walk those two mutts of his.'

Bri stared at the key hung by her front door, the key to Chase's house. The one he'd given her after the movie last Saturday.

'Thanks, that's really sweet of you. But I made a commitment, and I'll keep it. I don't mind taking care of the dogs. Honest.'

'You sure?'

'I'm positive. I kind of like them. Kiss Lainey good night for me, will you?'

'Sure.' Ross's voice dropped again. 'Think about what I told you, okay?'

'I will.'

*   *   *

And Bri did. All night and all the next day. Saturday night, she tossed and turned, still unable to clear her mind. Sometime in the wee hours of Sunday morning, she fell into a deep sleep. When she woke, sunshine streamed through her bedroom windows.

Oh, no! She'd overslept. The poor dogs must be desperate for a walk.

Gray sweats dangled over the arm of a chair where she'd tossed them. She pulled them on and struggled into a long-sleeved Pirates T-shirt. No time to primp. Not unless she wanted to clean up doggie puddles.

When she flew into Chase's house, the dogs met her at the door. She stepped in to retrieve their leashes, and memories nearly undid her. Memories of Chase and Lainey laughing. Memories of Chase's goodness. That day had been filled with sunshine, too. Sunshine that

158

reached her heart.

A splotch of pastel pink, vivid against the living room's neutral tones, caught her eye. Funny she hadn't noticed it yesterday. The folded note she'd written to Reeny lay wedged under the phone. From an ashtray beside it, the earring she'd lost on their first date winked at her.

Why had he kept them? She shook her head sadly. That streak of sentimentality, his marshmallow core.

She'd hit it right on the button Friday night. The roadblock in their relationship lay in front of her door.

But he'd deceived her by omission. If only he'd told her up front why he'd come to her rescue. If only her father had been honest and faithful. Her father . . . had been as charming and as attractive as Chase. A heartbreaker—in every sense of the word. They were two of a kind.

When she added in Chase's reticence to involve his heart, there it was. The end. To continue seeing each other would be asking for trouble. There could be no happy-ever-after for them.

The bulldog looked at her sympathetically and offered her his paw. The golden Lab offered her his leash.

'Well, Brianna Michelle, you can stand here and feel sorry for yourself, or you can take care of these frantic dogs.'

She opted for the latter.

Flawlessly trained, they walked at her side. General pranced and pounced, while Bull trudged stoically along. But both seemed to enjoy their time out.

*   *   *

Chase managed to catch an earlier flight. He unlocked the front door and stepped inside. Ah, home. Glad to be back, he loosened his tie and called his dogs.

'Hey, fellas, where are you?'

He dropped his suitcase in a corner of his bedroom. The house stood empty, but Bri had been here not too long ago. Her scent lingered.

When he'd phoned Ross yesterday, his brother said she'd insisted on keeping her promise to take care of the dogs for him. Why? Was it a matter of honor that she always kept her word, or did he dare read something more into it? Had she been as reluctant as he to sever the tie between them?

A quick backyard check confirmed the dogs were gone. Out for a walk. With Brianna. A slow smile creased his face as he decided maybe he should take a walk, too. Blow off the tension of traveling.

A block from the house, he spotted her. She hadn't seen him yet, so he stopped, waited, unsure how she'd react to him. Even a lukewarm reception might be hoping for too much. She'd been beyond angry the last time he'd seen her.

She looked gorgeous. In old sweatpants and a T-shirt two sizes too big, she made his heart beat double-time. Her blond hair haloed her head in the bright sunshine.

When she stopped to tie her sneaker, the dogs saw him. General gave one sharp bark of greeting. Chase raised a hand to silence his dog, but kept his distance.

He couldn't help himself. Common sense warned him not to get himself deeper into hot water, but his love of mischief won.

With one hand signal, he ordered the dogs to stay.

Obediently, they sat. She still hadn't seen him, and he didn't want her to. Not yet.

Brianna straightened. 'Okay, let's go.'

Both dogs refused to move. Bull sat on his rear and smiled up at her.

'What's wrong, Bull? You tired? Come on, we're almost home.'

Impatiently, she pulled on his leash, but the dog stayed put.

'What? You're just going to sit here in the middle of the sidewalk all day?'

No response.

'Well, you might not have plans for the day, but I've got tons to do, so let's go.' She tugged on his leash, but the animal wouldn't budge.

Exasperated, she ran her hands through her

long blond hair, then placed one hand on her hip. 'So what's up, Bull? You've been such a good boy. How come now you decide to act as stubborn and obstinate as Cha . . .' She sighed and her shoulders slumped. 'As me.'

She turned to his companion. 'How about you, General? Ready to go home?'

He met her words with a wag of his tail, but no other movement.

'What in the world's going on here?'

She knelt between the dogs and rubbed their ears. Bull's tongue flicked out and lapped at her nose. Giggling, she hugged him.

General, not wanting to be outdone, put his paws on her shoulders and gave her a wet kiss.

'You two are really being bad.' She laughed. 'Come on, now. We need to get back. Chase will be home soon, and believe me, I intend to be long gone before then.'

Chase caught their eyes and reminded them with another silent gesture to stay.

She stood. The golden Lab sat back down on his rump.

'Oh, no! General, what are you doing? Come on.' She yanked at the leash, clucked to him as though he were a horse. Nothing. He didn't move an inch.

'There's a big bone at home with your name on it,' she cajoled.

After a minute, she said, 'That doesn't appeal to you, huh? Okay, how about if I promise you a steak dinner?'

When the bulldog nudged her, she said, 'Yes, I'll fix one for you, too.'

Still, neither moved. She pleaded with the dogs to no avail. Her promises grew more and more outlandish.

Chase grinned. He watched her, envied his dogs as her hands caressed them. His breath caught as he remembered the feel of her touch.

She switched tactics and reverted to threats. Nothing.

By now, the sun, high in the sky, had heated things up. 'Come on, guys. You're too heavy to carry. Besides, there are two of you and only one of me. I'm dressed too warmly for this. I need to go home, hop in the shower, and change into something cooler.'

Chase's internal temperature leapt skyward at the mental vision her words created.

Out of sorts now, impatient at the delay, Bri stomped her foot. 'Okay, time to go. I'm hot. I'm frustrated. At this point, I'd even be willing to play slave to Uncle Chase for a day if you'd stand up and walk home.'

Unable to believe his ears, Chase quickly flashed his dogs the signal to get up.

With that, his pets, tongues lolling, practically leapt from their crouch and sprang forward to meet him.

Bri's shout of triumph turned into a scream of terror as she turned and ran smack into Chase's chest.

Startled by the blood-curdling shriek, he jumped back. Both dogs, cowards that they were, hit the ground.

'Jeez, Bri. Get hold of yourself.' His head swiveled, his gaze checking neighboring windows. 'Somebody's gonna call the cops.'

'Good.' Initial terror under control, her blue eyes flashed with anger. 'What are you doing here? You're not supposed to be back yet.'

'I caught an earlier flight.' He stuffed his hands into his pockets. He ached to grab her, pull her close, and kiss her senseless. But he didn't think that wise.

She glared at the dogs. 'Traitors.'

Then she tossed their leashes at him. 'Here. Finish the job yourself.'

Her narrowed eyes full of fury, she fumed, 'You did that, didn't you?'

'What?'

'Don't give me that innocent, holier-than-thou look. I'm not buying it. Somehow, you made the dogs stay put.'

When he opened his mouth to deny it, she held out a hand. 'No. Don't. I know you did.'

A guilty grin swept his face. 'Bri . . .'

'Uh uh. I don't want to hear any of it, Chase. You're too good at lying.' She rounded on the dogs. 'And you two, going along with him. After everything I did for you. Well, forget about the steak dinner.'

She shook her finger at the bulldog. 'And wipe that silly grin off your face, General.'

'That's Bull.'

'You're right. It is bull. All of it. And I'm done. Promise kept. I'm going home.'

'Aren't you forgetting something?' Chase spoke quietly.

'Forgetting something?'

'Yeah. You have one more promise to keep. I heard you. You stood right there and told these two that if they got up and went with you, you'd be my slave for a day. The dogs obeyed. They did what you asked, and now I feel obligated to make sure you keep your word to them.'

Incredulous, she stared. The seconds rolled by. Then, refusing to take the bait, she turned on her sneakered heel and walked away, nose in the air.

His voice filled with amusement, Chase called to her retreating back. 'Come on, Bri. I've always wanted my very own beautiful genie at my beck and call, ready to fulfill my every wish. You wouldn't disappoint me, would you?'

Back ramrod straight, she continued along the pavement.

His heart plummeted along with any hopes he'd harbored that she'd soften up and take pity on him.

'Okay, guys. Let's go home. Looks like we've been deserted.'

*   *   *

She detoured to Allie's house.

That depressed her even more. Hot and unkempt, she shook her head in disbelief. A vacuum stood in the front hall. She'd forgotten Sunday was her stepsister's cleaning day. Yet here she was, in the middle of her weekly housecleaning, looking like a million bucks. Not a single dark hair out of place, makeup perfectly applied, Allie wore an oatmeal-colored linen short set. A crisp, *ironed* oatmeal-colored linen short set. To clean in.

'Allie, you make me sick.'

The other woman raised an elegantly arched brow. 'Good thing I'm a doctor, then, huh? You're a little older than my average pediatric patient, but what the heck. Guess I can make an exception.'

She held the door open and stepped aside. 'So, why don't you come in and tell me what's really on your mind"

'Men. I hate them!' Bri tromped through to the kitchen and opened the fridge. 'Any iced tea?'

'Yep. Top shelf. Fresh this morning. Help yourself. Please.' Arms folded over her chest, Allie leaned against the doorjamb. 'You can pour one for me while you're at it.'

Bri filled two glasses with ice, then poured the amber liquid over it, listening as it cracked and popped.

Then she took a long, cool drink. One hand

propped on the counter, she held the cold glass to her warm cheek.

'Pour yourself a refill,' Allie said. 'Let's take them out back. I think we're probably going to have a long talk.'

'I'm sorry.' Tears swam in Bri's eyes.

'Don't be silly. This is what families are for.' She opened the back screen door. 'Come on. Let's sit in the fresh air.'

Outside, Bri gave her stepsister a hug. 'I love you.'

'I know.' She set down her glass and sank onto a lounge chair. 'Now . . . what's wrong?'

'Prince Charming.' Her lips quivered.

'Ah. I figured it might have something to do with him . . . and the bet he made with his brother.'

Bri's blond hair swung in her face as she turned to gape at Allie. 'You know about that?'

'Yep. The prince and I had lunch together the other day. No grand ball for me, mind you. Just the hospital cafeteria. We sure turned some heads, though.'

Bri's scowl deepened.

Allie's mocking tone faded. 'Sis, he loves you.'

She shook her head in denial, but Allie's dark eyes held her silent.

'Listen to me, Bri. I know you're hurting and you're angry. You have a right to be. No woman wants to find out she's been the object of a bet, that somebody took her out to win a dare. But that was only your first date. What about the rest?'

'What about them?' she countered.

'Come on. Be fair. He came back for more. And believe me, that's out of character for him. Nobody forced him.'

Unwilling to let go of her anger yet, Bri chose to argue the point. 'We kind of did . . . with the want ad.'

'Uh-uh.' Allie shook her head. 'He didn't have to answer that. You didn't have a clue who he was. Chase could have ignored the ad. But he didn't. He knew you needed him and he came to you.'

Bri thought about it. Allie was right. As usual. The first date had resulted from the dare, but not the second or the third. Nor the kisses they'd shared. She almost sighed. Those hadn't been part of any dare, although each and every one had issued its own challenge to her. And she'd lost.

She told Allie about Ross's call, what he'd said about his wife, the loss and pain the brothers had shared.

Her stepsister listened, then broached the subject of Bri's father.

Defensive, Bri tried to shut her out. 'I don't want to discuss him.'

'I know you don't, and everyone's always abided by your wishes. Maybe we shouldn't have.' Allie moved to the edge of her chair and leaned toward her sister. 'Because of that, you've never dealt with his death. After all these years, you still haven't come to terms with it. Despite what you seem to think, your father didn't deliberately leave you or your mother. Nor did he mean to mislead anyone. I truly believe that. I think he figured he had plenty of time to straighten everything out. But his time ran out. You can't let that dominate your life . . . or keep you from loving. It would break his heart.'

'He broke mine,' Bri whispered.

'I know, but he never meant to.' Allie slid onto her sister's chaise and wrapped her in her arms, cradling her.

'But what about my father's letters? The ones to that other woman?'

Bri thought of the sunny afternoon, so long ago, when Allie had found her, crumpled in a sorrowful heap in the hot, dusty attic, her father's letters to his lover in hand. Shattered, she'd lifted her tear-streaked face and explained. Allie had held her then, too.

Now Allie whispered, 'That's the day we truly became sisters.'

She nodded. 'I never told Mom I found them.'

'Maybe you should.'

'I can't.'

'Love's the most—'

Bri put her hands over her ears. 'I don't want to hear it. I've said it before, and I'll say it again. Love's a gamble, and someone's always a loser. Like my mom.'

'But you're forgetting that your mother and Dad have a good, strong second marriage. You need to open your heart, Sis. Let it heal.'

'I'm afraid to.' Her words ended on a sob.

*   *   *

A long time later, both sat wet-eyed and mopped at faces and noses with Kleenex.

'He wants a genie.' The words tumbled out before she could stop them.

'Pardon?'

Bri giggled, then hiccuped. 'Chase. He wants his very own genie-for-a-day to do his bidding.'

Allie eyed her sister. 'So, what are you going to do?'

'Take that step forward.' Her blue eyes gleamed with sudden mischief. 'I'm going to grant him his wish. And maybe fulfill mine at the same time.'

CHAPTER TEN

'This is the whole outfit?'

Allie nodded. 'That's it.'

Bri held the tiny scraps of sheer fabric in front of her, faced the mirror, and looked doubtfully at her reflection. 'Maybe I can't do this after all.'

'Oh, yes, you can.'

'Allie . . .'

'No. Don't you dare back down now. You can do this. Pay the man, and let's go.'

'You're getting awfully assertive in your old age.'

'Isn't that the truth? See what you have to look forward to?' Allie nudged her sister toward the counter. 'I know what you're doing. You're trying to antagonize me. It won't work. I'm not going to fight with you so you can blame me later because you didn't go through with this. Quit stalling. We still have lots to do.'

Bri sighed. This had seemed like such a good idea. Now, she wasn't so sure.

'What if he's not home?'

'He will be,' Allie said. 'I checked his schedule at the hospital today.'

'Maybe a different outfit.' Her eyes strayed to the racks of costumes.

Her sister shook her head. 'That one's fine.'

Bri held up the two pieces again and eyed them critically. 'Do you think I should try these on?'

'No.' Allie plucked the outfit from her hand and moved to the cash register. 'I'll pick up the tab for this one.'

All right. Fine. Bri made up her mind to go through with it, just to prove she could. Besides, it might be interesting at that. Very interesting.

Her chest grew tight as she thought about Chase, about being alone with him and what the night might bring. *Whew!* She fanned her face, then patted her chest. Her heart pounded beneath her hand.

Shopping bag in hand, she hopped into the car, and they forged on. Four blocks later, Allie's new red Porsche rolled to a stop in front of the deli.

Bri entered the little store first. Delicious aromas filled the shop and made her mouth water. The smell of fried peppers blended with the tang of tomato sauce and the aroma of freshly baked bread.

She inhaled deeply, appreciatively, then greeted the shop owner. 'Hello, Mr. Fabrizio. How are you today?'

'Bene, grazie. Molto bene.' Short and balding, he wore a huge white apron and a wide smile of welcome. 'I'm always wonderful when two such beautiful ladies come to visit.'

He covertly looked toward the door that led to the backroom. In a stage whisper, he said, 'Of course, don't tell Mama I said that.'

Louder, for his wife's benefit, he added, 'And my wife of forty-three years grows lovelier every day.'

A woman's voice rose above his. 'Girls, ignore him. He's an old man. What can I say? His eyes, they aren't so good anymore.'

Mr. Fabrizio laughed. The two bickered and

bantered all day long and obviously loved it.

'I have your picnic ready, Brianna.' He lifted a wicker basket onto the counter. 'It's all here. A nice antipasto salad, some of Mama's meatballs, a fresh loaf of warm, crusty Italian bread, and, of course, the lasagna. Pop it in the oven while you eat your salad. Ten minutes. Just till the cheese melts.'

He kissed his fingertips in a salute to good food. *'Delizioso!'*

Lifting the lid, he peeked inside the basket. 'Ah, yes. For dessert, Mama picked her biggest, juiciest strawberries and dipped them in chocolate.' He smiled widely and pulled a bottle partially out of the wicker carrier, then patted it. 'And, of course, the *vino.'*

His eyes sparkled. 'Special plans tonight? Someone very important, no?'

She smiled back. 'I hope so, Mr. Fabrizio.'

'Ah, well, you let me know, eh? I cater your wedding for you.'

She laughed. 'That's a little more than I'm shooting for.'

'You never know. Good luck tonight.'

'Grazie. Ciao.'

She hefted the basket and carried it to the car. 'Good thing we only have one more stop. There's not much room left here in this matchbox car of yours.'

'Yeah, yeah, yeah.' Allie slid into traffic and drove to the florist's. 'What kind of flowers did you order?'

173

'Actually, I got him a plant. White heather.'

Bemused, she asked, 'White heather? Why?'

Bri wiggled her brows and patted the harem costume at her feet. 'It means, "Your wish will come true." It seemed appropriate for a genie.'

'I think you're right.'

When they reached Bri's house, Shaylyn met them in the driveway, brimming with curiosity. 'So what exactly is going on here?'

Bri threw her younger sister an innocent look. 'Nothing.'

Shaylyn snorted. 'Right. Don't give me that. You have me dig up all the romantic music I can find and rush it over here. Something's going on. Prince Charming again?'

'Bull's-eye! Allie will explain everything, but you have to promise not to breathe a word of this to Mom and Dad.'

With that, Bri dashed off to take a quick shower and slather herself with perfumed lotion, leaving Allie to deal with their younger sister.

Fifteen minutes later, she stood in her bedroom doorway, tugging at the skimpy top. Her sisters nodded approvingly.

'Quit fussing with the outfit,' Allie said. 'I'll drive you to the good doctor's house.'

'You don't need to do that.'

'Oh, yes, I do. If I leave you alone, you'll change your mind. You can call me anytime, and I'll come get you.'

*   *   *

Chase rummaged clear to the back of the fridge. Nothing appealed to him tonight. Maybe he'd run out for Chinese. Or he could order in a pizza.

A carton of cottage cheese caught his eye. Just as he reached for it, the doorbell rang. The dogs barked and ran to answer it.

'Tell whoever it is that I'm not home,' Chase called after them.

Too bad they couldn't. He wasn't in the mood for company tonight. He needed to think, to get his head straight. Somewhere along the line, Brianna had taken over his every waking thought, not to mention his dreams. He didn't have a clue what to do about her.

When the doorbell rang again, he swore and shoved the cottage cheese back in the fridge.

'Coming,' he bellowed. 'Keep your britches on.'

When he yanked open the door and saw the britches in question, his knees turned to jelly. Absolute astonishment paralyzed him.

Brianna fell into the house, staggering under the weight of the basket.

'Close your mouth, Chase. And your door. Unless, of course, you don't mind your neighbors watching. I can assure you, several

175

of them have already seen me and are wondering what's going on. Your reputation is probably ruined,' she said breezily.

She set the basket, bag of tapes, and plant down on his breakfast bar, then turned to face him.

The full impact of her outfit hit him.

'Your mouth is still open, Doctor. You did say you wanted a genie, didn't you? Well, here I am.'

She raised her arms overhead and pirouetted, dancing around him. A bracelet of bells encircled each ankle and added music to her movements.

Speechless, he rotated with her. The outfit covered more than a bikini would have, yet somehow it seemed so much more provocative. And the gauzy creation was red. Red. He would always associate that color with her. That suit she'd worn the first day he'd seen her, the gown she'd dressed in for the ball. All red.

And now, this outfit. He swallowed. A strapless top, tied in front, covered the barest essentials. The bottom rode low on curvaceous hips and revealed her belly button. A tiny red jewel nestled within it and winked at him. Filmy, transparent material billowed around her legs. Bare feet, their toenails painted shiny red, peeked out beneath.

A fire, red-hot, started deep inside him.

Long blond hair, like a veil of molten gold,

flowed loosely over her shoulders, down her back. He wanted to bury his face in it.

Her fragrance, the one she always wore, swirled around her.

What was he supposed to do?

He didn't have a clue.

'Since you're not speaking, I assume you want me to read your mind, anticipate your wishes.' Her voice, low and sultry, stoked his fire.

She smiled, and her voice dropped to a whisper. 'I think I can do that.'

Chase nearly groaned as she moved toward him. She placed one hand on either side of his face and pulled his head down to hers. Their lips met. The kiss was deep, bone-melting. It fired the blaze within him almost beyond control.

When she pulled away, her eyes shimmered with passion.

'First, let's eat.' She spoke softly, her breath caressing his ear.

He nodded and swallowed again.

'While I get everything ready, maybe you could put the dogs in the yard. They won't mind, will they? It's a beautiful night.'

'Yes, it is,' he answered, finally finding his voice. 'An extraordinary night.' General and Bull romped with him to the door.

He stood in the backyard and looked up at the heavens. A few stars sparkled in the early evening sky. 'No lonely cottage cheese tonight, guys.' Unable to believe his luck, he took a deep breath and turned toward the house—and his destiny.

When he stepped inside, soft music issued from his stereo system. A white lace tablecloth lay spread on his living room floor, a low vase of fragrant white flowers in its center. A bottle of fine wine waited to be poured.

It hit him. This was all-out seduction. He'd never been on the receiving end of it before, but decided he liked it.

What had he done to deserve this? He grinned. It didn't matter. He'd just sit back and enjoy.

Bri stood at the kitchen counter. He walked up behind her and brushed the hair away from her neck. Then he dropped slow, gentle kisses along it, down her spine till he came to the barricade of her top.

Burying his face in the back of her neck, he slid his finger under the delicate material, trailed it around to the front till he touched the curve of her breast, felt her sharp intake of breath. His fingertips strolled from there down the front of her, along the hollow of her waist, to the top of the harem trousers. His finger brushed the jewel in her navel.

His lips moved to her ear. 'Do I get to make any wish I want tonight?'

She answered with a slight nod.

'Will my genie grant them all?'

Again, she nodded.

This time he did groan aloud. He turned her in his arms and claimed her lips. His hands roamed over her, reveling in the sweetness of her skin, the feel of her. He needed her. Right now.

She, though, had apparently decided to prolong his agony. She'd made big plans and wasn't about to hurry anything. Even if that meant he'd be half-crazy with desire before the night ended.

'Let's eat.' She led him to the table and knelt across from him. Then, she fed him.

He figured he'd died and gone to heaven.

A good while later, his appetite for food sated, Chase sipped his wine. Somewhere in the far recesses of his mind, it struck him that his living room looked like Bri's, stuff scattered everywhere. And he didn't mind a bit.

Then the song they'd danced to on their first date began to play.

He set down his glass and crooked a finger at his audacious, whimsical genie. She popped one last strawberry between her luscious lips and came to him.

They danced; their bodies melted together. His hand slid between them. With one small tug at the tie, her top loosened and fell away.

He stepped back, drank in the sight of her bare breasts. Absolute perfection. His mouth went dry.

What had begun as play now became deadly

serious. He couldn't wait any longer.

When their lips met, both knew the time for games had ended.

Voice raw, he said, 'Brianna, tell me if you don't want this as much as I do. I'm at the point of no return here. If you're going to pack up your things and go home, do it now.'

He drew back to look into her sapphire eyes. 'Otherwise, you're not leaving tonight.'

'Your wish is my command.'

Her words whispered through his brain, echoed and wrapped around themselves.

With that, he scooped her up in his arms and carried her to his bedroom. The bells on her ankle bracelets tinkled softly, reminding him of her seductive dance. He knelt on the edge of his bed, then gently laid her down. Slowly he lowered his body beside hers, ran a hand over the sheer pantaloons that covered the silky length of her legs. His lips touched heated flesh through the gossamer material.

When she sighed his name, he rose on one elbow and covered her lips with his. He paused to take a breath.

'Bri, I . . .'

'No.' She touched his lips with her fingertip. 'No words.'

When they came together, he knew that his life had just begun. The melding of their bodies was a coming home, full of tenderness and peace, a sense of belonging completely. Nothing had prepared him for this. Nothing had come close to the mind-blowing experience of making love to Brianna Winters.

He held her close, aroused her, pleasured her in every way a man could until she cried his name . . . and they became truly as one.

They fell asleep still wrapped in each other's arms.

*   *   *

When the phone rang, Chase woke to find Bri snuggled against him. His leg rested between hers. Intimacy had always scared him. Now, with Bri, he found himself treasuring it.

The phone rang a second time. He leaned across her to answer it. She turned as he did and her bare skin brushed his. He immediately wanted her again.

Somehow he managed a mumbled greeting, while his free hand lightly stroked her face. She placed a kiss in his palm.

Then his mind registered the nurse's words. One of his obstetrical patients had been admitted. A new life was eager to begin.

'I'll be right there.' He dropped the phone into its cradle and gave Bri a quick peck on the cheek.

'I've got to run.' Already out of bed, he hustled toward the closet.

'What's wrong?' She sat up, the sheet clutched around her. Blond hair tumbled over her shoulders.

'Nothing. This is part of my job, a good part, actually. Babies often decide to arrive in the middle of the night.'

'May I go with you?'

'I might be awhile. Labor is an unpredictable process.'

'That's okay. I don't mind. I'd love to go.'

'Get dressed then, honey.'

Her face fell. 'I can't. I don't have anything to wear. My genie costume's definitely not appropriate.'

He grinned. 'Oh, I don't know. I've seen some pretty strange get-ups at deliveries. I remember one dad who was wearing his wife's bathrobe. He'd thrown it on in the dark.'

His gaze traveled over her, took in the tousled blond hair that cascaded around her face and shoulders, the curve of her breasts barely covered by the sheet. He remembered the way she'd looked in her harem outfit.

'The plain, simple truth is that I don't want anyone else to see you in that costume.' His voice grew husky. 'Save it for me.'

'Why, Doctor, you're not jealous, are you?'

'Damned right I am.' And he realized that, as strange as it seemed, he'd never meant anything more in his life. Brianna Winters was his woman. He swallowed the lump in his throat.

'Let's see what I can find.' He dug around in his closet and came out with a pair of navy blue sweats and a white dress shirt. 'Will these work?'

'Sure will.'

In a matter of minutes they were dressed and on their way. At 2:30 A.M., no traffic clogged the city streets. When they arrived, he showed his ID and pulled the Jeep into the hospital parking lot.

Once inside, he led the way into the obstetrics wing and showed her to a lounge. 'You can wait for me here. I don't know how long I might be.'

'That's okay. Honest. I'll read a magazine, take a snooze, watch some late-night TV. Don't worry about me.' She gave him a quick kiss. 'Now get going. Some anxious parents-to-be are waiting for you.'

He snaked his arm around her waist for another kiss and drew her close, deepening it. Their tongues tasted, darted across one another's. 'I miss you.'

'You haven't gone anywhere, silly.'

'Yeah, but I know I have to. I'll hurry back.'

'Please do.' She blew him a kiss.

*   *   *

An hour and forty minutes later, Bri still wrestled with herself. Allie had been right. No need to lock herself away. But still, she'd decided to do this genie act as a lark, knowing there would be no harm in enjoying the moment. Two healthy adults taking pleasure in each other.

That's all it was meant to be.

But it had been more, much more.

Physically, making love with Chase ranked right up there with the very best life had to offer. And it had shaken her to her core.

Yesterday morning she'd been one hundred percent certain Chase Mitchell would never be part of her life. Now, less than twenty-four hours later, she seriously doubted she could exist without him.

Debonair, handsome, One-Date Mitchell.

Oh, boy. She was in deep trouble. How could she have known the impact one enchanted evening would have on her?

A light knock sounded on the waiting room door. When Bri looked up, a smiling nurse stood there.

'Brianna Winters?'

'Yes. Yes, that's me.' She set the dog-eared magazine she hadn't really been reading on the end table beside her.

'Doctor Mitchell sent me to find you. He'd like you to come see our latest arrival.'

When she arrived at the nursery, Chase, in his scrubs, waited there, a tiny blue bundle cradled in his arms. She pressed her face to the window, and he held up the newborn for her to see.

'He's beautiful.' Tears filled her eyes.

Chase winked. 'We don't deliver 'em any other way. Brianna Winters, meet David

Eugene Anderson.'

Chase placed his free hand on the nursery window. She laid hers against it, touching him through the glass.

And she knew.

She knew she needed his love, ached to have his baby, longed to bake birthday cakes for their own sons and daughters. She wanted a lifetime with a family of her own. With Doctor Chase Mitchell at the center of it.

CHAPTER ELEVEN

Chase banged on the door. 'Get up, damn it, and answer your door. We need to talk.'

Inside, footsteps shuffled toward him.

A rumpled and disheveled Ross opened the door, bleary-eyed. 'Quiet,' he whispered. 'You'll wake Lainey. What's wrong with you? Been drinking?'

'No, but that's not a bad idea.' He pushed his brother aside and barreled into the house. 'Got any coffee?'

'Not made.' Dressed in a pair of baggy boxer shorts, Ross rubbed his sleep-filled eyes.

'Make some, will you?'

'Sure, your royal pain-in-the-hiney. Your wish . . .'

Chase growled. 'Don't even say it.'

'What?'

'That's what started all this.'

Ross threw his hands in the air. 'I don't have a clue what the hell you're talking about, but I guess I'd better get that coffee going.'

While the percolator rumbled and burped, Chase explained the trick he'd played on Brianna with his dogs and followed with the story of last night—with some judicious censoring. He figured his brother was a big boy and could rcad between the lines well enough.

Coffee done, Ross poured two man-sized mugs full of the steaming brew and plopped them down on the table. Then he dropped onto a chair across from his brother.

'So what do you do now?'

'I don't know.'

'You love her?'

'Yeah.' The single word admission held both anger and reluctance.

'Have you told her?'

Chase shook his head. His hand moved to his chest, rubbed at the hurt there.

'Well, baby brother, the way I see it, you've got three choices.'

He held up one finger. 'You can walk away now and cut your losses—and probably lose the love of your life.'

A second finger joined the first. 'You can go along as is, and see how what happens next.

'Or,'—he stared hard at his brother—'you can grab this chance at happiness and run with it. Tell the lady you love her. See if you can talk her into spending her life with a worthless, bad-tempered scoundrel.'

Chase ignored his brother's insults. 'Do I really have those choices?'

'Probably not. Not if you really love her.'

He sighed, defeated. Pain ripped through him at the thought of walking away from his Bri. Nothing could hurt worse.

*   *   *

Brianna sat at her desk, absolutely, utterly miserable. Last night had been the most wonderful, the most perfect, night of her life. And today she felt wretched.

When they'd left the hospital, Chase asked her to go back home with him. She'd wanted to. Instead, she'd had him drive her to her place. It was late, and she needed to be up early for work.

He argued, said it was against his better judgment, but finally gave in and did as she asked. Big mistake. She hadn't slept another wink. For an hour and a half, she'd tossed and fretted alone in her bed, missing him, debating which had been her worst mistake—going to him in the first place or not going with him again.

Behind her hand, she yawned. Maybe a cup of coffee would help. As she stood to get one, her office door opened.

'Mom!'

'Hi, honey.'

'Is everything okay?' Panic stampeded through her.

Her mother had visited her at work only two or three times, and she'd always called first.

'Oh, everything's fine. Do you have a minute?'

'Sure.'

'We need to talk, dear, and I'm afraid if I put it off, I'll lose my nerve.' She closed the door behind her.

Uneasy, Bri waved her to a chair, then sat on the corner of her desk. A colored paperweight caught her eye. She picked it up, ran her hand over its smooth surface.

'You look terrible, Bri.'

Direct. That was her mother.

She wrinkled her nose. 'Gee, thanks.'

'I'm sorry, but you do. I expected to find you all smiles and happiness. Shaylyn told me what you girls were up to last night.'

'She didn't!'

'Yes, she did.'

'Argh! That snitch!' Bri paused. 'Did she tell you . . .'

'Everything, yes.' Her mother nodded and picked a small piece of lint from her skirt.

'Well, it's not really what you think.'

'It isn't?'

'No.' She faltered under her mother's gaze. 'Not exactly.'

'You did go to Chase's house?'

'Yes.'

'Dressed in a revealing, little harem costume?'

She replaced the paperweight to her desk blotter, but couldn't quite bring herself to meet her mother's eyes. 'Yes.'

'And your intent, if I'm correct, was to fulfill his wishes. All of them.'

Bri covered her face with her hands and mentally swore revenge on her baby sister. Silence seemed the best course, so she said nothing.

'I called Allie this morning. Wanted to see what she had to say about your Doctor Mitchell.'

'*My* Doctor Mitchell?' Curiosity overcame her indignation. 'What did she say?'

'Other than he has the best body on the staff and the most incredibly sexy green eyes?'

Brianna rolled her own eyes. Her older sister apparently had no more common sense than the younger one. Must be the shared genes from their father.

'She thinks he's one hell of a nice guy. Her words, not mine,' her mother added quickly. 'Shaylyn told me Allie drove you there.'

'Yes, she did,' Bri answered slowly, having a pretty good idea where this particular part of the conversation was headed.

'How nice of her to offer you a ride home— no matter how late.'

Bri nodded. Not a single hole opened in the

189

floor to offer an escape route.

'So, when exactly did you call her, dear? When did she pick you up?'

'Mom, this might be a good time to remember that old adage, "If you don't want to hear the answer, don't ask the question."'

Valerie Winters shook her head. 'No, honey, I don't think so. Something's happening here that I need to understand. This is different from any relationship you've ever been in. You always stay somewhat standoffish and distant.' She narrowed her eyes. 'No, don't give me that look, Brianna Michelle. We both know it's true. You never let any of the men you've dated get close, never really given them a chance, as far as I know.'

'I don't tell you everything, Mom.'

Her mother eyed Bri speculatively. 'But now you've taken the initiative.'

'I didn't really mean to.'

'Yes, you did, consciously or not.' She paused. 'Yet this morning I see fear and hesitancy. Why?'

'Mom, how can you ask me that after what Daddy did to you?'

'Your father never . . .'

'I read the letters,' she blurted. Her voice broke.

'The letters?' Confusion knitted her mother's brow, darkened her eyes. 'What letters, honey?'

Bri dropped into the chair behind her desk,

threw her head back, and closed her eyes against the pain. 'The ones he wrote to that other woman. The ones in the attic.'

Silence rushed in, as palpable a presence as a third person in the room.

When she opened her eyes, her mother's face had turned a pasty white. Alarm raced through Bri at her thoughtlessness.

'Mom, I'm sorry. So sorry. I shouldn't have mentioned them.'

'No, Brianna. *I'm* the one who's sorry.' She held up a trembling hand, brushed back a lock of still-blond hair that had fallen over her forehead. 'I had no idea . . . I thought those letters had been destroyed.'

'I found them in a box filled with old receipts and things,' Bri explained.

Mother's eyes found daughter's and held. 'I never meant for you to see those, had no idea you had. Why didn't you tell me?' She shook her head. 'Never mind. Now that you have, we need to talk about them.'

She sighed. 'Those damned letters. Still causing trouble. They're the reason you've kept yourself at such an emotional distance, aren't they?'

'Mom, if Dad couldn't be trusted, can any man?'

'John was a wonderful man, a wonderful father. But he had one major flaw. He was human.'

She frowned at her mother, not

understanding.

'Brianna, you've always viewed your father as a god. He wasn't. He was human just like you and me . . . and he could be just as stupid.'

Her mother stood, walked to her, and tucked a strand of hair behind her ear. Her hand rested on Bri's cheek a moment, then she turned and walked to the window to stare out at the city beneath her.

When she spoke again, her voice was low, not much more than a whisper. 'I loved him. He loved me. We had a beautiful little girl we both doted on . . . you. His company planned to start a branch in San Francisco and flew him there to work out some details. Before he left, we had a terrible argument, and I said some things I never should have.'

She turned, faced her daughter. 'I'm not making excuses for him. There are none to justify what he did. I am trying, though, to be fair, since he's not here to speak for himself.'

Once again she faced the window. Her fingers gripped the ledge. 'As it turned out, his business kept him there five weeks. That's when it happened.'

She walked back to her chair and sat down. Bri noticed she looked tired, older, than when she'd come in. Dredging this up had taken a toll.

'He confessed the whole thing to me the night he returned. Said he'd write to her, explain their fling had been just that. It was over.'

Bri stared. 'And you believed him?'

'I had to. Times were different. People didn't rush into divorce court the way they do now. And I'd promised to love him till death parted us. I did . . . and beyond.'

An unvoiced argument formed in Bri's mind, but before she could say more, her mother continued.

'I did some serious soul-searching, honey, and decided I wasn't going to throw away the love of my life, my happiness, because of one indiscretion. Had there ever been another, yes, in the blink of an eye. And your father knew that.

'We got through it, Bri. Possibly our marriage grew stronger for it, because we both realized how much it meant to us. Don't use what happened to me as an excuse to live your life without love. I haven't. I gave your father a second chance and I wasn't sorry. When I lost him, Bernard walked into our lives.' She fussed with her top button. 'Give Chase a chance, too. Don't punish him for your father's sins.'

Peace settled over Brianna at last. She knew her mother spoke the truth. So simple and so unhesitating, it could be nothing else.

All these years, she'd bottled up pain, anger, and fear. Why hadn't she gone to her mother when she'd first found the letters?

She knew the answer. She hadn't been ready, would not have believed her mother's explanation. Chase had opened her heart, had allowed her to accept the truth.

Doggedly, her mother, poise regained, returned to her earlier inquiry. 'Now, daughter, you still haven't answered my question.'

'Your question?' Bri's head spun dizzily as she tried to fully understand her mother's words.

'When did your sister pick you up?'

Eyes lowered, Bri doodled on her blotter. 'She didn't.'

'Oh?'

'Actually, Chase drove me home.'

Her mother pursed her lips. 'And would that have been last night or this morning?'

Extremely uncomfortable, Bri cleared her throat. She did not want to be having this conversation. Her mother waited, hands folded in her lap, the embodiment of patience.

Bri realized the futility of silence, so she answered, 'This morning. But it's not what you think. Well, actually I guess it is, but it isn't.'

Her mother didn't respond.

'Chase drove me home from the hospital about five this morning.'

'From the hospital?' Her mother's hand flew to her throat.

'I'm fine.' She grinned. 'We delivered a baby, Mom.'

'You delivered a baby?' Her mother's voice turned incredulous. 'Now there's an excuse I

194

haven't heard.'

'*I* didn't deliver it. I paced the waiting room floor like an expectant father. Obstetrics is Chase's specialty, in case Allie didn't tell you. That's what he does, Mom. He brings these incredible new lives into the world.'

The earlier excitement reclaimed her. 'You should have seen the baby, a little boy. David Eugene. He was beautiful, absolutely beautiful. Chase held him up to the nursery window for me.'

'Oh, Bri, honey. You finally found it.'

'What?'

'Love. Your father would be so happy. He adored you, his little Brianna Michelle. You were his pride and joy. It would have destroyed him to know how very much he hurt you.'

'He hurt you, too, Mom.'

'But I experienced it as an adult. More important, I loved him as his wife. That made all the difference in the world.'

'I loved him, too.'

'But as your hero. Sometimes it's hard to live up to such high expectations.'

'I love Chase.'

'I know you do, sweetie. I can see it in your face when you talk about him.' She patted her daughter's cheek. 'And I know I'm going to love him, too. Any man who can put stars like that in my baby's eyes has my undying gratitude.' Her own blue eyes shimmered with

195

tears.

Then a mischievous twinkle replaced them. 'That genie costume must have lit a roaring fire under him.'

Bri felt her face flame. 'You do know, don't you, that I may have to take revenge on Allie and Shaylyn?'

'Now, honey, it's all right. I can't say that I approve of . . . well, everything you planned, but I am glad you've finally found someone special enough to make you take that leap of faith. You've held a grudge against your father far too long, and you've let it stand between you and love.'

'Mom . . .'

Her mother shook her head. 'Now, now, don't *mom* me. It's about time someone brought you to your senses.' She got up to go, smiling fondly.

'Well, between you and Chase'—Bri walked her mother to the door—'I feel much better. I think.'

'I'm glad, honey. I wish you'd come to me sooner.' She patted her daughter's cheek. 'Try to get some sleep tonight.'

Back at her desk, Bri allowed herself another few minutes to digest what she'd learned, then another to daydream. With reluctance, she finally dug the top file from her basket and began wading through a tort case.

Two hours later, a disturbance outside the office door caught her attention. Now what?

Her door opened. A group of coworkers congregated in the hallway. They moved back, and she gasped.

The smile slid from her face.

'What in the world? General? Bull? What are you doing here?'

She stood and walked around her desk. Then she started to laugh. The two dogs looked positively comical. Both wore rhinestone tiaras, Bull's tipped cock-eyed on his round head. Whimsical sequin-covered gossamer wings sprouted from their backs. One of the General's wings was bent at an odd angle. And the crowning glory—pink tutus. As Bull waddled through her door, his tutu swayed back and forth fetchingly.

Bri looked from the pets to the office staff. 'Does anyone know what's going on?'

They all grinned and shook their heads.

Someone toward the back called out, 'I think one of them has a note for you, Ms. Winters.'

Her forehead creased in question. 'Bull. General. Come here, guys.'

Sure enough, she found a note pinned to the General's wing. She removed it and unfolded the paper.

Bri,

Cinderella's fairy godmother warned her to keep an eye on the time. I hope you'll do the same. At the stroke of twelve, look out your office window.

Love, your prince

She read the note again, aloud this time. *Love, your prince.* She hugged the note to her heart, not caring who saw.

A glance at the clock showed eleven fifty-eight. She threw open her window and leaned out.

Everybody scattered, determined to find a spot at one of the other windows. They wanted a front row seat for the rest of this unfolding drama. Nobody wanted to miss whatever would come next.

At exactly twelve noon, the bells of St. Mary's Cathedral tolled the hour. Their peals were nearly drowned out by the hum of a low-flying aircraft. The old biplane trailed a banner that read, *Marry me, Brianna!*

She squealed with delight and knelt to hug the two dogs. Then a noise behind her brought her heart to a standstill. She spun around.

Chase stood just inside her office, a diamond ring in his hand, his heart on his sleeve.

'I thought love meant hurt, Brianna, but I was so wrong. Love is far more powerful than fear. Tell me you'll spend your life with me. As long as I am, I'm yours. I love you. Marry me. Please.'

She flung herself into his arms. 'Yes, yes, yes.'

Stella asked, 'You're engaged, right? So you already asked her this question, right?'

'Yeah,' Chase replied.

He swept Brianna up and twirled her around the room to a burst of applause from her coworkers.

'But this is the happy ending. Can't have a fairy tale without a happy ending.'

We hope you have enjoyed this Large Print book. Other Chivers Press or Thorndike Press Large Print books are available at your library or directly from the publishers.

For more information about current and forthcoming titles, please call or write, without obligation, to:

Chivers Press Limited
Windsor Bridge Road
Bath BA2 3AX
England
Tel. (01225) 335336

OR

Thorndike Press
295 Kennedy Memorial Drive
Waterville
Maine 04901
USA

All our Large Print titles are designed for easy reading, and all our books are made to last.